"There's a whole lot of new land out West . . ."

"You're thinking about that 'prairie-ocean' again, Johnny. I can see it."

"And why not? It's getting a little too civilized around here. Why, just look at yourselves. Few years back, you had a small spread and a one-room cabin. Now you've got more than a hundred acres to work, and a real house with whitewashed clapboards and shutters painted red even!"

"God has been good to us," I smiled, "but painting the shutters red was *my* idea. Adds a nice touch to the place. And did you see Pa's new windmill?"

Johnny shook himself, kind of frustrated-like. "Don't you see, Meg? It's all part and parcel of being hemmed in. I've a yen to see some Indians and buffalo, take the books out to those'll be needing them to keep away the snowed-in winter melancholy. Hmmm, maybe even pick up with one of those wagon trains organizing out of Independence. Just imagine the glory of being on one of those treks, with a wagon full of books." His eyes were shining as he looked somewhere out where I couldn't see, couldn't reach.

"Not yet, Johnny," I said, worried some for him, some for myself. "Your pa needs you."

"Don't I know it?" He looked at me then and reached for my hand. "Don't worry, Meg. I'm not about to leave him. He and the books are all I've got in this world. Except maybe—you."

"You've got the Lord smiling down on you, too, Johnny, and don't ever forget it. Bible says, 'My God shall supply all your needs according to his riches in glory by Christ Jesus.' When the time is ripe, you'll have what you need."

"And when will the time be ripe for me to have *you*, Meg?"

FROM THIS DAY FORWARD

Kathleen Karr

Serenade/Saga
BOOKS
of the Zondervan Publishing House
Grand Rapids, Michigan

FROM THIS DAY FORWARD
Copyright © 1985 by The Zondervan Corporation

Serenade/Saga is an imprint of
The Zondervan Publishing House
1415 Lake Drive, S.E.
Grand Rapids, MI 49506

ISBN 0-310-46942-2

Edited by Nancye Willis and Anne Severance
Designed by Kim Koning

Printed in the United States of America

85   86   87   88   89   90   /   10   9   8   7   6   5   4   3   2   1

*For my parents, Stephen and Elizabeth Csere,
who gave me love, and a love for books*

Part I

THE FARM

CHAPTER 1

I FIRST SET EYES on Johnny Stuart when I was ten years old. I was in the front yard drawing water from the well to fill the animals' drinking trough when I heard the clip-clop and rattle of a horse pulling a cart 'round the bend and through the trees to our place. My mouth was open to yell that company was coming when I saw the boy leading the old white mare. About three years older than I, he was dancing along beside the horse, locks of curly black hair framing his laughing, mischievous face. My open mouth finally remembered to shut itself. It was love at first sight.

"Ma! Pa!" The bucket clanged to the bottom of the well.

"Maggie! You forgot to feed the swine! I can hear them snufflin' clear inside the cabin!" Pulling up his suspenders, Pa came to the door, then stopped to watch the progress of the tiny caravan up the incline to the cabin.

Ma peeked out from behind him, wiping floury hands on her apron. "Gracious! Who could that be?

Don't recognize the wagon. The peddler's not due for another month."

The wagon, more like a gypsy caravan, with brightly painted sides and roof, creaked to a halt near the well. The boy, silent and serious now, walked to the back, unlatched a small door, and hauled out a disheveled old man who swayed for an instant, then pulled himself upright, doffed a mangy hat revealing a head of sparse, stringy gray hair, and bowed in the direction of my parents.

"Allow me to introduce myself. Charles Stuart, purveyor of books, inspirational and educational, moralistic and fanciful. At your service." He hacked and spit with a fine sense of direction into the trough, then added, "And this is the son of my old age, John Stuart."

The boy aped the bow of his father, then asked, "Might I water our Mabel and loosen her up to graze a bit while we palaver?"

My parents were still staring, dumfounded. I found my tongue first.

"Our pleasure." Then I ran over to help with the horse.

Ma, still wiping her hands in awe, remembered herself. "Sure, and we get little enough company out here. Will you stay to take a meal with us?"

"Your kindness is overwhelming, madam. We accept." So saying, the old gentleman assayed another bow, failed midway, and keeled over with a plop. The boy dropped Mabel's harness, and raced over to help his father into a sitting position.

"Take no mind of Pa's weakness, folks. I'm afeard the payment for his last set of books has done him in proper. A good meal and he'll be back to rights again."

My pa was moving now, helping the old man up, walking him to the rough wooden bench by the cabin door. "What kind of payment could do this to a man?"

Johnny just grinned. "Farmer fifty miles over the mountain bought ancient copies of Dilworth's *School-master's Assistant* and *New Guide to the English Tongue*. Paid for them with three jugs of home brew. Wouldn't touch the stuff myself, but Pa always was one for getting his money's worth. Just let him lean there a bit."

"What's 'home brew'?" I asked innocently.

Ma and Pa just looked scandalized.

The boy sidled over to me. "Your name Maggie?"

I drew myself up to a full four and a half feet and pulled a bit self-consciously at my carrot-red braids. "Pa and Ma call me that, but my true name is Margaret McDonald."

He stared at me a moment. "Sure like your freckles. And never saw such blue eyes. May I call you Meg?"

My mind toyed with the new appellation and approved. It was somehow ladylike. "You may."

"Good. You may call me Johnny."

"Maggie!" My father was roaring.

"Yes, sir?"

"Feed the livestock!"

"Yes, sir!"

My two little brothers who had been hiding behind Ma's skirts soon got up their courage and trotted after Johnny and me. He wanted to know if they were twins.

"Near enough. Abe was born first, Aaron near as spit to nine months later. And they do look alike." I sighed. "Guess red hair and freckles just naturally run in the family." Then, curiously, "Where's your ma?"

He looked suddenly sad. "Don't know. Pa just says she disappeared soon after I was born. Said he had to bottle-feed me himself, just like a runt." He brightened up. "Pa and I, we get along fine. Don't need any women. He taught me to cook, and read. . . ."

We had finished slopping the hogs and were in the chicken pen now. "You can read?"

"I should hope so!" He stopped, then looked at me. "Can't you?"

"My pa says womenfolk don't need to know. When a schoolmaster came through last winter, he wouldn't let me go to learn. Said my mother needed me more."

"Can't read!" he said with some awe. "Let me show you something." He dragged me from the hens to the funny old wagon, stepped up on one of the wheels and fussed with a hook at the top. Suddenly, the whole side let down. "Look."

There sat rows and rows of books, their leather and cloth bindings gleaming softly in the sun. I pulled in my breath, then let it out, easy. Suddenly I knew I wanted to read more than anything. "Teach me, Johnny."

He thought a minute, then said, "All right, but let's get away from the cabin."

He took me off to a bare patch of ground near the forest and found a stick. Then he began scratching strange-looking symbols into the dirt.

"The alphabet, Meg. You start with the alphabet."

I sat in the dirt all morning and shaped and sounded letters to his instruction. He had just put together three letters, *M-E-G*, and said, "*Meg.* That's how your name looks."

When the dinner bell sounded from the cabin, I was loath to rise. "Trouble. That's what I'll get mighty soon from this."

He smiled gaily, his sparkling black eyes meeting mine. "We'll see," he promised. Then, "Come on! Race you!"

They were already seated 'round the rough board table: Pa, heading up one end, on the chair he had made with the stiff arms and back; the boys and

Johnny's father, on the bench 'round the far long side; Ma, standing by ready to serve. Pa gave us a look and we sat. On account of company, Pa's grace was longer than usual. I peeked at Johnny's father when Pa got to the new part, about "protecting us from Satan's brew." I was gratified to see that he looked much perkier and was eying Ma's stew with longing. Finally Pa got to the amen and we all dug in.

After a few bites had brightened him visibly, Johnny's father started in talking, quite elegantlike. He went on about his books and his travels and, before I knew it, I'd plowed through five cobs of new sweet corn. I didn't understand all of it, but got the part about how they went to Philadelphia every winter to restock their wagon with books, then were out on the road again for the rest of the year. Occasionally they'd be invited to stay somewhere for a spell and tutor the local children. Here, old Mr. Stuart stopped a bit to refill his plate and look longingly at Pa. Pa took no heed of the broad hint, just dug further into his vittles.

"I'm sure you understand, Mr. McDonald, the benefits of reading and writing. . . ."

"Sure do. Read my Bible to the family every night, and had cause to write a letter just two years back."

"Ah, then you appreciate the merits of the King's Book."

"It's the Lord's Book I'll be talking about."

"Of course, I was referring to the King James Version."

"Be there any other?" Pa asked suspiciously.

"There's the Latin and the Greek. I've some fine samples in my wagon. . . ."

"Don't take to no heathen Bibles here. Got *my* Pa's Book that *his* Pa brought himself from Scotland after 'The Forty-five'."

"Your grandfather was a Jacobite, then. Loyal to the Stuart kings."

"Yes," Pa said. "After the movement was crushed, he left Scotland. And his Bible's good enough for me."

"Of course, of course. Its nuances are perfection. And the glory of its poetry. . . ."

Pa looked suspicious again. "Don't know about poetry," he said stubbornly, "only about the Lord's words."

"Would you be interested in a fine book of sermons by a minister, himself of the kirk, to augment your readings?"

"Bible's good enough for me." The way Pa said it, we knew the subject was closed.

"Ah, yes. Then what about these fine children of yours, sir? Surely you'll want them to be able to read the Lord's words as well? I have out in my wagon the newest thing in aids to reading for the young, complete with fine moral lessons." He reached for a piece of bread and looked up hopefully.

"What might that be?"

"Why, *McGuffey's Eclectic Reader,* of course. By none other than William Holmes McGuffey, a fine preacher of the kirk, descended from Scotland like yourself and myself, grew up amongst these very Ohio hills. Just printed last winter."

"Would he be the one who used to preach around here some years back?"

"He would. Teaches now over at Miami University in Oxford. He's been compiling his *Reader* for ten years there."

Pa was visibly considering. "Seems to me I heard him at a camp meeting before I started courting Mrs. McDonald. A fine speaker."

"Indeed. And just think! It's possible to have his excellent influence in your very own home! As an adjunct to that of yourself and the Bible, of course."

Pa scratched his ear, a sure sign of hard thinking.

13

"Might be something in what you say. Abe and Aaron ain't gonna be three forever."

I held my breath, inwardly praying for Pa to purchase *McGuffey's Eclectic Reader*. I was almost blue with the effort by the time Pa scraped back his chair and rose.

"Guess you talked me into looking over your wares, Mr. Stuart." He gave the old man a sudden look. "My old Pa had a framed likeness of Prince Charles Stuart he hung over the mantel for years, right above his musket. Willed it to my sister when he passed on. You bear a kind of resemblance to Prince Charlie, God save his soul. Know you that?"

"It's been whispered to me, indeed it has, Mr. McDonald. I never knew my father, but my mother came from Skye, she did. Never said a word. But a man can dream. Especially an old man like myself."

Pa looked odd for a moment. "How old be you?"

"Lost track after eighty, Mr. McDonald."

Pa, standing now, raised and drained his mug of cider, then threw it on the hard dirt floor. "Over the water!" was all he said.

I watched, mystified, while Ma wiped her eyes with her apron. Then I poked Johnny next to me. "What is happening?"

He just grinned knowingly.

Pa went out and bought *McGuffey's Eclectic Reader*. I stood and waved goodbye till I could no longer see Johnny leading Mabel past the bend in the road. After that it didn't rain for two weeks and I spent every spare moment hovering over that dry patch of dirt near the woods, memorizing Johnny's alphabet.

CHAPTER 2

IT WAS HARVEST TIME and I was eleven before I saw Johnny leading the old white mare 'round our bend again. Mabel looked older than before, and more worn out, but when Johnny hauled out his father, the old man looked the same as ever. Not another wrinkle had been added to his already wizened appearance. I held my breath, afraid Johnny had forgotten me. He looked older, taller, but he moved with the same grace, and the same fire danced in his eyes.

Johnny led Mabel up the rise, calmly unharnessed her, and turned to me. "'Lo, Meg. You've grown some. How's the alphabet coming?"

I could have hugged him, but instead stood there, poking at the dirt with my toes. Finally he looked down. I'd spelled "Johnny" in the dirt and he let out a whoop when he deciphered it. I went then to ring the bell for Ma and Pa to come out of the fields. Pa came round from the back of the cabin first.

"What in tarnation's going on, Maggie? The sun's not set yet and I'm afraid the rains may come tonight. We're not near done with the harvesting . . . Stuart!"

Johnny's father had by now pulled himself together sufficiently to greet Pa. "Your servant, sir." Maybe he *was* a year older. He had a little trouble straightening his back again after the bow. Could he really be near a hundred? I'd been worrying over that for a year. Nobody lived that long. Except Methuselah and the other old-timers in the Bible. Pa had taken to reading about them after the Stuarts' leave-taking last year. Also, unaccountably, he'd read a lot from the book of Kings. There'd also been mutterings for a while about Culloden, where the Jacobites had met complete defeat. I'd had to grill a lot of acquaintances at camp meeting last fall to begin to understand about the Royal Stuarts. Wasn't sure I followed it all completely yet.

My pa took another look at the book peddlers, then glanced at the ominously darkening sky—storm dark, not night dark was coming on. "Listen, Stuart. Your boy there looks strong enough. Let him help me try to finish the scything, and you can stay for the night. As for yourself, make yourself to home in the cabin. . . ."

"With thanks, good sir. If it pleases you, I shall also attempt to entertain your sons with some stories. Might hasten your work along."

Pa brightened visibly. "Good. Then Maggie can come help, too."

"Just let me check baby Charlie in his cradle, Pa, and I'll be right along." Charlie had appeared about two months back and thus far hadn't put too much strain on the household. Took to sleep like a duck to water. I tiptoed into the cabin and peeked at the sleeping babe. He was breathing deeply and peacefully, making little sucking motions with his mouth. Right nice.

Then I rounded up Abe and Aaron and set them on the floor near the door where old Mr. Stuart was propped up against the post. He'd brought a small volume from his wagon and, as I set off toward the fields, I could hear him say, "Now then, young gentlemen, it's high time you heard about Mother Goose." If it weren't for the wheat and the storm, I would've sidled right back to hear him myself.

Johnny was already swinging the spare scythe, and I could tell he'd had some practice. I walked up behind, gathering the wheat into bunches. God must've been looking over us, 'cause though the sky kept lowering, it didn't rain none, just kept getting darker. After a few hours it was pitch dark and we were still scything and collecting. My stomach and sore back told me it was long past suppertime, but Ma and the rest of us were needed more in that field. It was only when Abe came running out to say that baby Charlie was yowling his head off that Ma stood up, stretched, and headed back to the cabin. We'd finished the scything now, but Pa was scratching his ear.

"What's the matter, Pa? Should I go get the horse and cart to start loading the wheat?"

"That's just it, Maggie. Blackie pulled a tendon this afternoon and can't haul for a few days."

Then Johnny spoke up. "There's Mabel, sir. She should be rested up now, and though she looks old, she's still a good Conestoga out of Pennsylvania. Best draft horse ever bred."

Pa looked mighty relieved. "Thanks, boy. Let's go harness her up." He looked at me. "Keep sheaving, Maggie. The good Lord's holding off that storm, but He won't keep it back forever."

I straightened up to peer into the night sky and was rewarded with a long rumble of thunder. "Yes, Pa."

It was after midnight when we got the grain stowed in the barn and dragged ourselves into the cabin. Lightning was flashing through the sky, and the first drops of rain felt cool on my head. Ma had fallen asleep in the rocking chair by the fire, with baby

17

Charlie drowsing at her breast. Old Mr. Stuart was rolled up in blankets by the far wall, and the boys were tucked in up in the loft. I ladled up some of the vegetable stew from the pot hanging on the crane over the fire and served it to the three of us. Johnny's head was drooping, but he managed to eat his serving before putting his head down on the board table. Pa looked at the two of us.

"Get you up to sleep, Maggie. I'll put the boy in a blanket on the floor."

I just made it up the loft steps, collapsed into the soft hay with a quick evening prayer, and remembered nothing further till morning.

When I woke, it was raining. I lay and listened to the heavy beat on the roof for a minute, before the thought hit me: *Johnny is here!* Least I hoped he still was. Scared silly for a moment that he and his father could have gone off already, I raced down the loft steps, lost my footing and tumbled to the hard floor. When I looked up, Johnny was grinning down at me.

"I powerfully admire that descent. I truly do."

Before anger could take over from my shame, he hauled me up. I looked around. Ma was smiling at me from her rocking chair and even baby Charlie seemed to gurgle. It was all right.

Ma spoke up. "Your Pa's out in the barn with Mr. Stuart, arguing over politics and threshing. The boys, too. Get yourself some breakfast, then you and Johnny can go off for a bit. The chores will wait. You worked hard last night, girl."

Smiling my pleasure, I launched into a bowl of porridge and cream, finishing it to follow Johnny out into the rain. He led me to his wagon, right by the back door.

"Thought you might like to see where we live."

I glanced around at the snug quarters, taking in the

two bunks on one side, the tiny Franklin stove at the front. "It's right cozy."

"Yup. And snug in a storm, too. When it's nice, we cook outside, over a campfire, but when the weather's bad, we can just pull over and come in."

There was a little window on the side opposite the bunks by the stove, and he showed me how they had fixed up a small table that could be levered up and down from the wall. Under the bunks was a long drawer filled with their clothes and bedding, and a lantern and pots hung from the walls, filling all the remaining space. He reached to the upper bunk and pulled a book from under his pillow. Almost reverently he showed it to me.

"I've read all the usual books Pa stocks, but every winter he tries to buy a little variety—for my education, he says. Just got to this one and it is mighty special."

I looked at the title page and managed to spell out "Washington Irving."

"There's a story in here . . . well, it's exciting. I would dearly love to share it with you."

"Please," I breathed.

We spent that rainy morning reading *The Legend of Sleepy Hollow*. We were just moving on to *Rip Van Winkle* in high anticipation, when I heard Pa yell "Maggie!" The two of us jumped away from that book and out the door of the wagon faster than a crow can caw.

"Yes, Pa?"

"The threshing. Remember?"

"Yes, Pa."

Johnny and his father stayed three days; Johnny, seeing us through the threshing, his father, lounging nearby in the warm barn, regaling us all with fine tales of President Jackson and worries about the new president, Martin Van Buren.

"I don't understand," said Pa at one point. "I heard 'Old Hickory' hand-picked Van Buren to follow him."

"He did that, Mr. McDonald," answered Johnny's father. "But Van Buren lacks Jackson's spark, his way with the people. There have been many complaints about Andrew Jackson's 'spoilage' system, but when he had his first inauguration, he opened up the White House to *everyone*. Brought in a several-ton cheese, set it right in the middle of the ballroom, and everyone who came in helped himself to a bite. Oh, yes, indeed. Even the Whigs could have supped off it, but it was a bigger bite they were looking for."

Pa resumed his threshing, chewing that over some then, "But did not Jackson near get us into war with the old country?"

"Nonsense, man. He was a bit outspoken for a diplomat, but he always stood up for America. You would not have our sailors impressed again, and British soldiers on this soil?"

"Never! I may dream of Scotland from my grandpa's tales, but I reckon the soil is much better here."

"Even so. The Lord does work in strange and marvelous ways," commented old Stuart. "I expect if it were not for The Forty-five, we'd all still be starving in Scotland."

This was more talk than I'd heard in years, and I kept my ears full open to try to grasp it all as Johnny and I worked alongside Pa. Questions I knew I could not ask, or Pa would turn off his sudden stream of conversation. Best we were quiet, so he would forget our presence. I waited for more, but just then Ma called me to come help with the supper.

That night Johnny and I sat by the fire, speaking in whispers, lest we disturb the sleeping children. I showed him my *McGuffey's*, carefully unwrapping it from the bit of cloth I kept it tucked in to protect it. I could recite all of the words by heart, and made

20

Johnny giggle by doing so: "This old man can not see. He is blind. Mary holds him by the hand. She is kind to the old blind man."

"But however did you get your father to allow you to study it?"

"First I did it by stealth. But he caught me and gave me a whupping. Then Mother quietly pointed out that although she could not read, many's the time she wished she could so that she might study the Lord's words as well as my father. She said that surely the Lord had not meant His words for men only, and what would happen if something terrible occurred to Pa and none of us could read those words? Pa relented then, and said I could study some, but not so's it would interfere with my chores. I have been most careful not to aggravate him."

"We've got McGuffey's third and fourth readers out in the wagon. Pa got them straight off the press this winter."

"No!" I said breathlessly.

"How we going to get your Pa to buy them?"

We began to concoct plans and strategies in whispers until Ma finished up with little Charlie and lay down in the big bed on the far side of the cabin, where Pa was already snoring.

"Maggie! Get up to sleep now!" Her whisper was loud, and Pa grunted and turned over.

"Yes, ma'am."

The rains finally stopped and Johnny and his father made preparations to be on their way again. Pa bartered some of the new grain, a dozen eggs and a couple slabs of bacon for the new *McGuffey's*. I stood by, watching the Stuarts load, helping to fill up their water bags, big bloated-looking leathern ones that hung from the outsides of the wagon.

When Pa's back was turned I noticed Ma sneaking a fresh new loaf of bread and a small jar of her best raspberry preserves into Johnny's hands. Johnny had been admiring those preserves for three days now, and the silent smile of thanks on his face lit up even Ma's eyes for a moment. Then Ma ran back into the cabin in answer to little Charlie's call, and Johnny stood facing me for a moment.

"Study hard, Meg, and next year I'll bring some more good stories."

I wanted fearsome hard to look into his eyes then, but something kept my own staring down in the mud. "Yes, Johnny." He touched my arm a moment, and I raised my eyes in time to see him scampering over to lead the horse and wagon out of my life once more.

"God go with you, Johnny!" I suddenly yelled. He waved an arm in answer and was gone.

"Come, Maggie, I'll need some help to change the poultice on Blackie's foreleg." Pa's voice was strangely gentle. Maybe he had an inkling of how I felt. Maybe he'd had a friend once.

"Yes, Pa."

CHAPTER 3

IT WAS STRAWBERRY TIME and I hadn't near expected them yet when the Stuarts' wagon rounded the bend in my twelfth year. I had finished slopping the pigs and was hanging onto the fence around their pen, dreamily admiring the new litter of piglets, when Johnny suddenly ran up beside me. I just stared.

"My Pa had a yen to try a new route this year. Wanted to see Cincinnati. 'S'posed to be the Boston of the West. Wasn't anything but pigs, though."

"Pigs?" I asked, still loath to believe the vision before me.

"Yes. Cincinnati people nicknamed it 'Porkopolis.' They have no garbage men, just let the pigs roam through the streets eating anything in sight."

"What's a garbage man?" My feet were frozen in the rungs of the fence, unable to move.

"Never been to a city, have you?"

"Never been anywhere but here and autumn camp meeting, sixty miles northeast over to Locust Grove. A regular town they've got there. A church, a school, a general store. Takes us near three days to get there,

23

with Blackie hauling the wagon. Usually spend the first night with the Campbells, though Pa never has felt comfortable there. Can't understand why. Seem nice enough people. Their children's all grown and gone off, though. Spend the second night bunked with the Millers. They're a German family from Pennsylvania. Got a daughter my age, Hildegarde. Mighty nice seeing Hildy once a year, though it doesn't hold a candle to your coming, Johnny. . . ." I stopped my flow of words, feeling suddenly a little awkward again. "Sorry, wandering around like that. Guess I don't get a chance to talk to people much. And what *are* garbage men?"

He just grinned, leaning on the fence next to me. "Well, in most big cities, like Philadelphia or New York, they hire men with wagons to haul away the garbage people throw into the streets. Usually take it to the nearest river to unload." He wrinkled his face as if remembering the smell. "You've got a right neat farm here, so I guess you wouldn't understand. In cities, even on some farms, the stench is horrible."

"Pa makes us bury everything unfit for the animals. Says if we just let it sit about, it'll bring the flies worse and poison the well."

"Your Pa's a smart man."

I climbed down the fence then and smoothed my gingham dress a bit. It was getting short, almost up to my knees, but mostly I didn't mind. Made it cooler when the heat came on. Then I looked up at Johnny. Had to look up at him. He must've added three inches over the winter. His homespun shirt sleeves were rolled up over his elbows in the late spring warmth, and I could see muscles beginning to bulge in his arms. Funny how I never noticed them before. Suddenly I felt very sad.

He put a finger to my chin and pushed it up so I had to look at him. "What's the matter, Meg?"

"You're almost all grown up, Johnny! Will we still be friends?"

He laughed. "You're getting there, too, Meg. A few more freckles, too, I see. Of course we'll still be friends! Look here, I left my pa at the cabin. Young Abe and Aaron saw him coming and besieged him for more stories, like last year. Your ma sent me to you with these."

I looked at the two wooden buckets he'd set down on the ground.

"She said if we filled one with forest mushrooms and the other with strawberries, she'd fix up something nice for supper. 'Course you'll have to teach me which mushrooms to pick. Leave the choosing to me, and we'd all be dead by morning," he chuckled.

"You've never picked mushrooms?"

"Nope. Not one of Pa's talents. Although I have helped myself to a cabbage or two from a farmer's field on our journeys."

"Johnny! They'll put you in jail for a gypsy!"

"We've been called worse, by some, but it's a good life wandering around." He'd handed me a bucket, picked up the other, and taken my free hand to start toward the woods.

I looked at Pa's fields, spreading out to the west. Practically seventy acres of his tract were cleared now, all by his own labor. I'd watched him sweating at it every free moment since I could remember. Pa had always said that the land and God were all that mattered. If you had land, you were somebody in this world; and if you had God, you were somebody in the next.

"Don't you ever have a yen to stop roaming some day, settle down on your own piece of ground?" I couldn't resist asking.

He followed my eyes around the spread, stopping a moment to take in the new hilly piece Pa had just finished fencing up as a pasture for the horse and cow.

After he was halfway done with that one, Pa'd judged it too rocky for plowing, so he'd left a few strands of trees for shade. It was right pretty the way our little stream wandered through it. Pa was even contemplating picking up a young steer or two to fatten on the grass. Said he'd wait till camp meeting this year. There was always some animal-trading going on during the last day.

"Can't say that I do. I admire the sprouts coming up in the spring." He pointed at the acres of wheat, oats, and corn beginning to poke up through the furrows of ground, his eyes taking in their expanse to the far wall of forest, then going back to the little two-acre kitchen garden behind the cabin. "And I'll be delighted to eat from it come harvest time, but I'll never be the man to stand behind the plow. My Pa says it takes all kinds to make the world, and the frontier could use our kind of sowing as well."

We started to walk again. "I never thought of it that way."

"Brought words to you, didn't we?"

"Yes, I can read now. But you still don't know how to pick mushrooms!"

Johnny just grinned, then followed me into the new greenness of the woods. And he would've had that bucket filled with toadstools if I hadn't been with him every moment. We never did get to the strawberries that morning. When we got back to the cabin, Ma had two pie crusts ready for the little beehive oven built into the brick chimney next to the open fire.

"Where've you been? Never thought you two youngsters would get back in time for the dinner cooking. Now hurry and get those mushrooms clean."

"You going to put mushrooms in a pie, ma'am?"

"With a little milk and egg custard. Family gets weary of constant porridge and stew, morning, noon and night. My ma wasn't afraid of a little experimentin', and neither am I."

Johnny sat by the table and watched me chop the mushrooms, followed me as I threw them into a big cast iron pan and fried them up with some butter and onion over the fire. Finally they were deemed ready, put into the crusts, and topped with the custard. After they were a few minutes in the oven, old Mr. Stuart poked his head in the cabin door.

"Does my nose deceive me, madam, or is that a *tansy* I smell baking?"

"Guess you could call it a 'tansy' if you like. My family never took to the bitter herb part, though my mother used it at the Easter time in memory of the 'bitter herbs' of our Lord's trials. Other times of year, I call it a pudding. Comes out right nice with bits of ham in it, too."

Johnny's pa was almost drooling, and I guess Ma saw that as easy as I, for she told me to ring the bell for Pa, and set the table to rights for dinner. Then she bustled over to the oven to check on her puddings with the long wooden pie peel. Finally Pa came and we all sat down and waited for his grace. Little Charlie was crawling around underneath the table, and every so often let out a nasty cough. Pa seemed to take no notice, just carried on praying. After the amen, Mr. Stuart paused before launching into his pudding.

"Master Charlie had that cough long?"

"Off and on since before spring," said Ma, looking worried. "Thought the change of season would loosen him up some, but it hasn't yet."

Mr. Stuart chewed a bit contemplatively. Had fewer teeth than last year, I noticed, but he seemed to be gumming down the pudding nice and smooth. "Got something in the wagon might be of assistance."

Pa looked up. "Haven't got a doctor tucked in there somewhere?"

"Next best thing, sir. I have Dr. Jonas Rishel's *Indian Physician*—a complete treatise on the causes and symptoms of diseases which are incident to human nature, with a safe and sovereign cure for them. Johnny!"

"Yes, Pa?"

"Go fetch a copy. If I'm not mistaken, young Charlie's got the croup."

Johnny shoveled another bite into his mouth, then ran out to the wagon. He reappeared quickly to hand a slim cloth-covered volume to his father. Stuart put down his spoon and examined the book carefully, then apparently satisfied, located the appropriate page and began to read:

" 'Croup. This disease consists of an inflammation of the mucus membrane of the windpipe, occasioning the secretion of a very tenacious coagulable lymph, which lines the windpipe, and obstructs respiration.' "
He paused and looked up to see Mother staring in horror. "That just means, Madam, that Charlie's having some trouble breathing."

"Oh."

He continued. " 'This disease is most incident to children, and usually prevails in the winter and spring, occasioned by a cold, moist atmosphere.' "

"*Has* been a wet spring," ventured Pa.

Everyone was staring at old Mr. Stuart now, eating at a standstill.

"Shall I continue?"

"Might as well," I commented. "Food's gonna get cold anyhow." Pa gave me a dirty look.

He started in again. " 'Symptoms: Respiration becomes difficult, attended with wheezing and a shrill cough. Face is sometimes livid, and by turns flushed; great thirst and restlessness . . . ' Er—umm—I think we can dispense with the rest and get on to the cure."

Ma had picked up little Charlie by now and was giving him loving and fearful looks in turn.

28

" 'Remedy: Take one handful of fresh chamomile, one handful of saffron blows, either fresh or dry, and three ounces of fresh butter. Simmer them together over a moderate fire, till the chamomile and saffron flowers become crisped. Give a teaspoonful of this oil every twenty minutes, till it affords relief. (This dose for a child one or two years old.)' " He peered at Charlie across the table. "Looks near enough to one to me." Then he looked at Ma. "Got some chamomile and saffron blows, Mrs. McDonald?"

"Hanging dry from the rafters in the loft, along with my other herbs. Chamomile makes a good tea for upset stomachs." Ma looked at me. "Maggie, straightaway you finish your meal, you go up and bring down a good handful."

"Yes, ma'am." I got up to do it right away. I knew there'd be no peace in this house till Charlie swallowed his first dose.

As I climbed the ladder I heard Ma say to Pa, "Jamie, maybe you'll be considering the purchase of that *Indian Physician* from Mr. Stuart. It's just by the grace of God he was here to listen to Charlie's cough today. It might be some help to us for the winter ills."

I didn't hear Pa's answer, but guessed it was in the affirmative, for Ma was smiling when I got back down and put the chamomile and saffron blows on the table. Then I helped myself to more of the mushroom pudding while old Mr. Stuart got up and began to supervise the cooking of the medicine.

Little Charlie had been almost forgotten on the floor while everyone, even Pa, sat around to watch the proceedings. The baby started in coughing again, so I picked him up and cuddled him some. A cute wee thing, he was, the only one of us children who hadn't picked up Pa's red hair. Charlie's was yellow, like Ma's—a fine crop, too. And it had a bit of curl to it. Wished some of that curl had been handed on to me. I sighed. But that was just vanity speaking. A blight upon the face of the earth was vanity. That's what Pa always said. Guessed I'd just have to get over it. Surely didn't want to be a blight upon the earth. Locusts last year were bad enough, ate nearly half of Pa's crop 'fore they filled themselves. I giggled then, and Johnny gave me a look.

"What's funny?" he hissed.

"Just thinking about vanity and locusts."

He looked mystified.

"Never mind. Ma's got the dose ready now."

I propped Charlie up in my lap and Ma came over with a spoonful of wicked-smelling stuff. She poked it tentatively into his mouth and we all watched Charlie's face. His nose wrinkled up, his eyes took on a look of disbelief, and he tried to spit it out. Sure didn't taste like mother's milk to Charlie, but we finally got it down, then Ma picked him up and set about to nurse away the bad taste. I started to clear up the table and Pa and Mr. Stuart wandered outside. By the time I was done, Charlie had fallen asleep and Ma tucked him into his cradle. His breathing seemed a bit easier and Ma looked relieved.

"Will Johnny and his pa stay the night, Ma?"

"I don't see why not."

"Can we go and pick strawberries now?"

She was obviously somewhere else, for she only nodded a bit absentmindedly, with another glance at the baby. Johnny was already at the door with the bucket. We raced out together across the clearing. We found a few strawberry plants near the edge of the woods, but soon had them picked clean. I plunked the last berry into the pail, which only had a thin covering on its bottom, then looked up to see Johnny gazing speculatively at the woods.

"What is it, Johnny?"

"Ever see a map of the state of Ohio?"

"What's a map?"

He looked bemused. "A map is a picture of the land

on paper. Shows you where the mountains are, and the roads, and the towns . . . and the rivers." He looked into the woods again. "Had an idea this morning, when we were picking mushrooms. Came to me again just now. Cincinnati's on the Ohio River, near the western part of the state. And across the river is Kentucky. Pa and I traveled out this year from Philadelphia, across the state of Pennsylvania, then south and west through most of Ohio, to Cincinnati. Then we turned around due south, southeast and traveled about seventy-five miles till we got to your place. Went along the Ohio River most of the way, then inland last few miles. Seems to me the river's got to be somewhere beyond these trees."

"Pa never said anything about a river nearby."

"Your Pa keeps his eyes on the path to heaven, and his feet firmly on his own ground. Don't think the river'd mean much to him if he didn't own a piece of it."

"What does the river look like, Johnny?"

He looked at me as he chose his words carefully. "Take the little stream running through your place. Make it as wide as your father's fields, sometimes wider. Then make it almost as deep and fill it with bountiful fish. On top of it put a few boats, floating or sailing downstream, with the flow of the water. That's a river."

I sighed aloud, my mind filled with the image. "Sounds right beautiful."

"Magnificent, the Ohio is. And a wonder it is, too, to see it filled up with Easterners on flatboats, keelboats, even rafts, all piled high with their belongings. All headed further west." His eyes took on a faraway look with the words "further west."

"Sure you haven't got some gypsy in you, Johnny Stuart? I can see the travel-craving in your eyes."

"Maybe. But I'm not the only one. Thousands and

31

thousands of people float down that river all the time. A sight to see."

"Well, why not?"

"Why not *what?*"

"Take me to see the river."

"I'd love to, but. . . ."

"But what?" I never was one to shilly-shally.

"Ought to get your pa's consent. And ought to start at daybreak. I'm not sure how far it could be—and there's the getting back."

"All right. We'll ask Pa tonight at supper. Maybe he'll let you stay another day. Your pa looks like he could do with a rest."

It was Johnny's turn to sigh. "Yes, he has been getting tired more easily lately." He looked around. "Let's get on with the berry picking then. Where's the next patch?"

So I took Johnny around the perimeter of the farm, following the plants. After an hour or two Johnny sat down and popped a few berries into his mouth.

"Seems to me it would be easier to pick up some of these plants and take them back to your kitchen garden. Then you wouldn't have to go traipsing all over the place, hunting for them every spring."

I was stunned by the new thought. "But they wouldn't be wild any more."

"What's wrong with that? If you cultivated them and gave them a little water now and again, you'd have more berries. Probably bigger ones, too."

"But you're not even a farmer!"

He smiled at my proprietary look. "Read a few agricultural books. Pa keeps them well stocked. They're his biggest seller next to the inspirational ones. You could do the same with raspberry and blackberry bushes. They'd make a pretty border to the rear of the garden, too."

I thought about all the scratches and mosquito bites I'd gotten crawling through the woods after these delicacies. Suddenly it sounded good. "I'll take it up with my pa. And now we'd better fill this pail, or they'll be asking what mischief we've been up to all afternoon."

With the now-heavy pail between us, we finally wandered back to the cabin near suppertime. My mind was whirling with new ideas about rivers and berries and the world beyond. The evening star had just come out in the darkening sky as we neared the homestead. Johnny looked up and started in muttering something.

"What's that?"

He was suddenly shy. "Just a little poem about the stars. "

"Tell me, please."

He coughed a bit, then started off in a deeper voice—funny how his voice seemed to keep coming and going up and down like that this spring—"Twinkle, twinkle, little star, How I wonder what you are. Up above the world so high, like a diamond in the sky."

Well, after he'd got done explaining what a diamond was, I guess he thought the poem was spoiled. But I made him say it again, trying to memorize it. Then Ma rang the supper bell and we headed in.

Pa was in high fettle after the grace. Little Charlie'd had more medicine and seemed better, so Ma was in good spirits, too. We had a right friendly meal, then Ma put a bowl of the fresh strawberries on the table and we all poured sweet cream over them for dessert. Pa started in talking first before I could get out any of the questions I was bursting to ask.

"Took Mr. Stuart into the woods today for a piece, Ma. Out towards the west to that little lake tucked in there."

I looked up in surprise. Would wonders never cease? Pa had never mentioned a lake before.

"Mr. Stuart's been filling me with some mighty

33

interesting ideas. You know how you're always wishing for some fresh meat, 'stead of smoked and salted always?''

Ma nodded.

"Ice! the answer is ice!"

Ma and I both looked perplexed.

"Back East, the Yankees in New England are harvesting ice from their ponds and lakes in the winter, storing it up in 'ice houses,' selling it all over the world to keep things cool and fresh.''

I just had to put in my two cents. "But ice melts, Pa.''

He gave me what could definitely be called an icy stare. "Listen to the child. Teach her to read and she thinks she's educated. Spend more time with the Lord's Book, girl, and less with your high-flown ideas and you'll learn the proper respect and silence a child should have.''

"Sorry, Pa.'' I cast my eyes down to my strawberries and shoveled in another spoonful. Luckily, I was instantly forgotten for his new idea.

"So, I build a little stone room, mostly underground, and, come winter, fill it with ice cut from the lake. Pack sawdust from my woodpile around the walls and ice slabs to further delay the melting. When it comes pig-slaughtering time, we put a couple haunches in there to test. Fresh pork roast in April, or June even.''

Mr. Stuart piped in, "And ice is very therapeutic for fevers. Not to mention cuts and burns. Why, a little chunk of it in July could save someone's life. I read in the papers that a piece of ice did just that in Calcutta, India. A piece of Massachusetts ice shipped near around the world in a clipper cooled the fevered brow of an Indian maharajah.''

Now this was getting interesting. Whatever was a "maharajah''? Sounded wickedly exotic.

"Don't forget ice cream, sir,'' interrupted Johnny.

"What's ice cream?" Even Ma craved an answer to that one.

Johnny looked at my pa, suddenly remembering he spoke out of turn. "Sorry, sir."

"That's all right, boy. What is ice cream?"

"Pa treated me to it in Philadelphia last winter, but it would be unbelievably delicious in the heat of summer." He paused, remembering. "You grind up a bunch of ice and pack it around a container of fresh sweet cream, sugar, and any kind of flavoring you can think of. These strawberries, for instance. It comes out soft and cold. Nearest thing to heaven I ever tasted." He looked at my father quickly. "No blasphemy intended, sir, but I'm sure the Lord put it in the mind of man to make for our refreshment. A little earthly reward for man's travails, you might say."

"Time enough for that in the next world!" Pa grumped, but I could see the idea tickled him. Young Abe and Aaron spoke up then, almost in unison, a rare occurrence at the dinner table.

"Please, Pa. We're old enough now to help. We can find the stones and carry them for you, and chop up ice and. . . ."

Then Ma pitched in. "I hardly think it can be wicked, Jamie. The ingredients are all the Lord's own. You'll just be putting them to a slightly new use. . . ."

Even Pa could tell when he was surrounded. "We'll see," was all he would say.

As it was obviously time to change the subject, I launched into the river and the strawberry cultivating.

Pa finished his dessert and looked at me. "Seems a powerful lot of new ideas 'round this house today. Yes, I know about the river. Was down that way when I was surveying the boundaries of our land when Ma and I first got married. No, you may not go there. It's over ten miles and there's no clear path. I'll not have either of you lost in the forest. As for the berries . . . if you wish to take charge of the project, Maggie, I have naught to say against it." And he leaned back into his chair, decisions made.

"Excuse me, sir?"

"Yes, Johnny?"

"My father could use another day of rest before we get back on the road. If we have permission to tarry another day here, and if I help your daughter with her chores tomorrow, may we go to see the lake? I've some fishing rods in the wagon, and perhaps a few fresh fish might be nice for your supper. . . ."

Pa thought for a bit. "All right, boy, but mind the chores get done properly before you go traipsing off."

"Thank you, sir."

As my father rose to saunter out back to take his evening air and check the livestock, I gave Johnny a grateful look. He had pulled a concession out of defeat, and I never had gone fishing. I helped Ma clean up, then dragged Johnny out to help haul in firewood to bank the fire for the evening. Then the chores were done and the younger children in bed. I was still wide awake, though. Johnny and I looked at each other with the same thought. He spoke first.

"If we lit the wagon lantern, we could read a bit. My pa will be happy to camp down by the fire here. Says his old bones need more warmth now, even on fine nights like this."

My Ma hadn't missed this exchange. I looked at her pleadingly. I could see her sizing up Johnny, with his new growth and all, but apparently she decided in his favor, for she nodded yes. "But not too late, Maggie. You've got a full day ahead of you tomorrow if you'll be thinking of catching all the fish in that little lake!"

I gave her a hug, then we went out to the wagon. And my, but it was cozy there sitting next to him. He'd pulled a book from under his pillow again. It was another writer, Walter Scott, a Scotsman, he told me with a grin. And such adventures his Rob Roy had!

Johnny kind of summed up the beginning for me on account of it was a little slow-moving, he said. Then he jumped right into the middle of it. We sat huddled over the book till neither of us could keep our eyes propped open further. Only then did I say good night and went back to the cabin and my loft, to dreams of distant Scotland's Edinburgh, a real city I could almost touch with my eyes closed. Not to mention heather-covered, craggy hills, and my wild ancestors, dressed in the plaids, dashing about those hills, fire in their eyes.

Ma had to yell me awake next morning, but when I remembered the day, I rushed down the ladder fast enough. Johnny and the boys were already finishing their porridge, and I sat down to my steaming bowl, exclaiming over the sprinkling of strawberries Ma had thought to top it with. Always had a nice touch, Ma did. I gave her a special smile, then gulped it down.

Johnny and I rushed through the milking and feeding, finally currying Blackie. Couldn't see how a farm horse needed currying every day, but Pa always said that if you did God's creatures proud, they'd do proud by you. And Blackie did seem to enjoy the attention. Finally got away by offering him one of the last of the fall's turnips. Pretty dry now, but Blackie whinnied with some appreciation. We went next to Johnny's wagon, where he carefully climbed to the top and removed two long sticks tied down to the roof. I examined them carefully, from the length of twine attached, to the little hooks at the end.

"What're they?"

"Fishing rods, of course."

"That all it takes to catch them?"

"These and a few juicy worms." He led me to the kitchen garden then and burrowed about a bit until he'd hauled up a dozen or so worms, then carefully tucked them into a little leathern pouch hanging from his belt.

Back at the cabin, Ma handed Johnny a satchel to put over his shoulder.

"Since it's some distance to the lake, thought you might like to take your dinner with you," she smiled. "Packed up some bread and cheese. Lake water should be fit for drinking."

"Oh, Ma, thanks!"

"You, young lady, had better catch some fish. I'll be doing the washing today and will count on them for dinner."

"Yes, ma'am!"

We were out of the cabin, running across the fields, passing Pa.

"Be careful of those seedlings, Maggie! No sense in destroying the crop."

"Yes, sir. No, sir."

Finally we were beyond, at the border of my world. As we set off through the canopy of green woods, I felt exhilarated. A whole day of freedom with Johnny! He seemed to sense my feelings as well, took my hand with a smile, and I followed him.

We'd gone maybe a half-mile when suddenly the trees opened up and the land came to a little rise. We climbed that rise and looked down on the prettiest little lake. Sun glanced off its surface and I watched a fish jump out to catch a low-flying bug.

Johnny laughed. "So it does have fish! Probably too many. And we're going to catch some of those lazy creatures today. Come on, let's find a good spot."

So we clambered down the rocky slope and took a slow walk around the water. Altogether the lake was probably about three or four acres in size, kind of narrow where we had met it, then stretching out in length toward the west.

Johnny finally chose two small boulders jutting out a bit over the edge as the best place, and we settled down to do some fishing. He pulled a knife out of a bit of sheathing connected to his belt, then dug into his pouch for a worm. I must say I was a bit squeamish about the baiting part, as he called it, but since he carved up the worm, I figured I had to help out, too, so I gingerly connected it to the hook, like he was doing. Then he showed me how to gently fling the thin twine into the water.

"What do we do next?"

"Wait."

"That's all?"

"Yup. You kind of keep a firm hand on your pole—not a death grip, Meg!" He loosened up my fingers. "Just hold it gentle-like. And if you feel anything tugging at it, you pull it up slow and easy, trying not to scare the fish away. You want his mouth to get caught on the hook so you can pull it in."

"Poor fish!"

"Why? That old fish is just an opportunist, like us. It's going after the juicy worm. If the fish can eat the worm, why can't we eat the fish?"

I started in pondering that, but suddenly felt a tug, and not so gentle, either. "Johnny! Something's . . ." I rose from my sitting place to get a better grip on the situation. Then the creature on the other end of the line gave a sudden lunge, pulling me off balance and toppling me into the lake below.

The water was frigid, but only about three feet deep. Course it took me awhile to figure out the depth, and when I finally got to my feet, sputtering with anger, I looked up to see Johnny laughing his head off. Now I never have been one to take humiliation lightly. Maybe my red hair's got something to do with that, maybe not. I spat out a mouthful of lake water and glared at him. He finally set down his rod and reached out a hand for me. I took it with a small smile, gave it a good yank, then watched in satisfaction as Johnny plunged into the water next to me.

When he finally came up he was still laughing, even harder, so I just naturally started in, too. When we stopped for air, Johnny gulped down hard, then said, "You've still got the rod, Meg!"

I looked down, and sure enough, there was that death grip, holding firm.

"Don't just stand there dripping. Pull in your fish!"

I looked at the rod dumbly for a moment, then gave a tentative tug. Something pulled back hard. I tugged again, and so it went until a glistening fish was flopping about us.

"What a beauty!" Johnny removed the gear from my hand and hauled the booty up to the rock. "It's a bass. Must be five pounds!"

I watched as he set about dealing with it. Then he picked up our gear and started moving off.

"Where're we going?"

"Got to find another spot. Just hope our swim didn't scare every fish in the lake."

So we found another rock further down the lake in the sun, where we sat drying off and rebaiting the hooks. Only after Johnny had pulled in two more, and I, with more grace, another, did he suggest lunch. By the end of the afternoon I had learned the mysteries of gutting and scaling fish, and we set off for home with over a dozen.

Johnny had strung them on two lines, but even so they got mighty heavy till we saw our farm clearing open up before us. Ma poked her head over her wash ropes, took one look at the two of us sauntering, proud as peacocks across the fields, and yelled to Pa.

"Jamie! Better get up the smokehouse fires. There's more fish coming than we can eat tonight!"

We supped royally that night, all of us off that first five-pounder that had pulled me into the lake. The others had been big, too, but none so big as this one. Ma just dunked him in flour and fried him up in a little butter with a dash of salt and pepper. Never tasted anything so sweet. Abe and Aaron were green with envy and begged to be allowed to go fishing, too.

Pa just looked at them for a while, then said, "Well, a little fresh fish on occasion ain't a bad thing. If Maggie will take charge of the trip, I might be able to rig up three poles, and maybe make some hooks out of a few spare nails out in the barn." He looked then at me.

"Be glad to, Pa."

Wouldn't be the same as fishing with Johnny, though. Nothing was the same as something done with Johnny, but it would still be pleasant. Have to keep the boys out of the lake, for sure. None of us had any swimming experience. The boys were jiggling up and down on the bench in excitement, and I could see by the look in their eyes that I had just risen some in their estimations. Nothing wrong with that, either.

As it was the eve of the Sabbath, Pa lazed around the table some after the eating was done. I cleared it off, then brought Pa's Bible over to him. He liked to make more of an occasion of the reading on a Saturday night. Pa thumbed through the book, thinking a little, then I saw him light up as he hit on the obvious passage for the day: "And it came to pass, that, as the people pressed upon him to hear the word of God, he stood by the lake of Gennesaret."

I knew right off he'd chosen the fifth chapter of Luke, and was mightily pleased.

And saw two ships standing by the lake: but the fishermen were gone out of them, and were washing their nets. And he entered into one of the ships, which was Simon's, and prayed him that he would thrust out a little from the land. And he sat down, and taught the people out of the ship. Now when he had left speaking, he said unto Simon, Launch out into the deep, and let down your nets for a draught.

I closed my eyes, and thought about the great multitude of fishes that broke the net, and opened

41

them in time to hear Pa finish with, "Fear not; from henceforth thou shalt catch men."

Pa closed the Book then and looked at me. "The Lord brought you those fish today, Maggie. Never forget that." He got up and went outside. Old Mr. Stuart sat picking at the few teeth he had left.

"Getting a little chilly tonight. Guess I'll bundle up by your fire again."

Ma put the youngsters to bed and Johnny and I headed out for another meeting with Rob Roy.

When the Stuarts pulled out in the morning, Pa stood clutching the *Indian Physician,* and I, Johnny's copy of *Rob Roy.* Never believe for a moment that Pa bought my book. Fact is, it was a present from Johnny—hard-won, too. Old Mr. Stuart had given his permission, but then Pa needed to be convinced.

"Be kind enough to accept it, sir, as a token of thanks for your hospitality," old Mr. Stuart had started in.

"Don't need any heathen works cluttering up my daughter's head, thank you, sir."

"Ah, but it's not a heathen work, sir! It's written by a true Scotsman, and a noble one, as well. Have you never heard of Sir Walter Scott?"

"Can't say as I have. Be he an ancient, or still living?"

Old Mr. Stuart scratched his ever-thinning white hair. "Well, I guess you could call him a deceased contemporary. Heard that he died about six years back. Not before putting Scotland on the literary map of the world, though, with his fine stories. This one here is practically history, gussied up some, about that fine old Scot leader, Rob Roy. I really can't conceive that it will hurt the child. More likely to help give her a true appreciation of our mutual ancestors."

Pa thought hard. "Well, maybe she can have it,

then, but I'll take you to task for it next visit, sir, if there be any ill effects."

"You have my word, sir." And Johnny's father creaked up the front of the wagon to take his place on the little seat there.

"Maggie!"

"Yes, Pa?"

"Run and get an extra bucket of oats for Mabel."

"Yes, Pa!"

Then they were gone and I ran up to my loft to tuck *Rob Roy* with my other treasures.

CHAPTER 4

IT WAS PAST HARVESTING, even past autumn camp meeting in early October, and I had almost given up on the Stuarts' coming when we saw them next.

I was sitting on the bench in front of the cabin before supper, making a corn-husk doll for Charlie. I'd already tied together about fifty husks, and the doll was just about finished. Charlie was running back and forth in front of me, asking "Done, Mag, done?" His talking was coming along right well, but he had some trouble with long words yet, so always called me 'Mag.' Charlie heard the horse first. I could see his little ears kind of perk up. Then he pointed down the dirt road.

"Com-ing, com-ing," he crooned.

First I thought it was the overdue peddler. And just in time, too, for Ma was down to her last needle and had clean forgotten to restock in Locust Grove, what with the excitement of Pa's giving her a little extra money to spend on pretty cloth at the general store. Pa had had a good year with the farm, had gotten together with some of the other local farmers and shipped a couple big wagons full of grain back East for hard cash. Now he was talking about starting in to build an addition to the cabin in early spring, and maybe even covering the logs with clapboard on the outside, just like the fine houses in Locust Grove.

Ma had been pleased, of course, but said that with all the growing going on in this family, we could all use a new set of clothes. We'd been sewing ever since camp meeting—when I had been baptized—and now the windows had a pretty set of curtains as well, kind of floating gaily from the twine that held them up. I stopped my musing when I saw the colors of the wagon peeking through the trees that were beginning to look bare now that most of their leaves were gone.

"It's Johnny and his pa!" I yelled.

Ma came running to look, and the boys and I raced down to meet them. Even before old Mr. Stuart was completely unloaded, I could see that they all looked tired, even Johnny. I helped to unharness Mabel, then gave Johnny a keen look as he stood there, wearily rubbing his chin.

"Johnny! You've got whiskers!"

He grinned. "And you've got—" he stopped. "You've got some new growth, too, Meg."

I glanced down toward my chest a bit self-consciously. Things had seemed to start popping this past summer. Ma had been pleased. Called me her "little woman" now. Wasn't sure what all I thought of the new developments yet, but guessed it was just a natural part of growing up, that and my becoming a real believer. I glanced up and his eyes met mine. We both smiled.

"Looks like you could use a good wash-up, and your pa, too."

"Thanks. It's been a dry fall, and water a bit scarce between stops. Let me just help Pa up to the cabin."

I finally gave his pa a good scrutiny. Wasn't happy with what I saw. I looked at Ma and she had the same look in her eye. The old man had aged more than we expected. She was already after nursing him up, I could see.

"You just lean right next to me, Mr. Stuart, and we'll have you in the cabin and refreshed in no time."

"My pleasure, madam," and he tried a little flourish of his broad-brimmed hat, then gave up on it and hobbled with Ma into the house. I stood with Johnny, watching.

"Your pa looks poorly, Johnny. . . ."

"I know. That's why we took the trip so slow this year. I was hoping a few days stay with old friends would perk him up some. I'm really glad we made it before nightfall. It's getting unseasonable cold, and there's the smell of snow in the air."

I gave the air a tentative sniff. "Maybe. Been dry so long I guess it's got to come down somehow." I walked over to the well and started in drawing up fresh water for Johnny's washing. Then I stood and stared while he looked into the bit of mirror Pa had hung over the basin just outside the door.

"Guess a shave wouldn't hurt." And he lathered up with our chunk of pig's grease soap, picked up Pa's razor and started in.

To say I was transfixed with awe might be an understatement. Probably might've made a fool of myself by pointing out that he hadn't *all* that many whiskers yet, but Ma saved me by yelling out for me to bring in some water for Mr. Stuart.

She had the old man sitting in the rocking chair by the fire, and was warming up some apple cider with herbs for him to drink. My, but he looked old and tired. This year I could almost believe he was a hundred. I edged up with my bucket, then took a cloth, wet it and washed the travel dust from his face. He sighed, closed his eyes, and just let me continue. His face had so many tiny wrinkles it looked like one of our apples after a long hard winter in the root cellar.

"Take off his boots, Maggie, and let him soak his feet a bit in the bucket. Does a soul good to wiggle his toes in fresh water every now and again."

"Yes, Ma." I unlaced his boots and peeled off a pair of very prime socks. His eyes were still closed, so I held them away from me a little and gave Ma a questioning look.

"Rinse them out back with some soap, girl, and we'll let them dry near the fire tonight."

"Yes, ma'am."

By the time I got out back, Johnny was finished with his ablutions, all except for his feet. "Take off your boots, too, Johnny. Long's I'm washing socks, might as well have clean feet to go with 'em."

He looked a bit bashful about it, but did as I asked. I noticed all four socks seemed to have more holes than wool left in them, so figured I'd just do a little mending on them after they'd dried. Johnny stuck his feet in a bucket of water as well and watched me work.

"Sure is nice to have a woman look after us now and again."

I looked up from the scrub-board. "Your story's changed some from a few years back, Johnny. Seems I remember something about not needing any women around."

He rubbed his cheek where he'd knicked it a bit with Pa's razor. "Maybe you're right, Meg. It's harder with Pa not being able to do his share, I guess. Anyway," and he changed the subject, "I do like your new dress. Shawl's pretty, too."

I looked down at my new winter woolen dress. "Just finished sewing it up. I knit the shawl, too." I was proud of that. "We got the wool this summer from the peddler. Traded it for a passel of my

47

strawberry preserves. Ma let me dye it this color blue.''

"Matches your eyes to a T.''

I blushed. "Remember your idea about the strawberry plants?'' He nodded and I continued. "Straightaway after you left last trip, I started in with the transplanting. Pa gave me an extra piece of land beyond the kitchen garden for the berries. Tended them like babies, then added blackberries and raspberries, too, after their season. Had more than we could eat of any of them this year, so I started in making preserves. Then I ran out of pots, so Pa brought me a new batch just three weeks back at Locust Grove. He's just finished building me a jelly cupboard, too, to match Ma's pie safe. Want to see it?''

"Sure do,'' he smiled.

So I finished rinsing the socks and he trotted barefoot into the cabin after me. I hung them up to dry by the fire, then looked around the room. Sure did seem to be getting smaller all the time. The big table was still in the center, with Ma and Pa's rope bed over by the far wall, covered with a pretty quilt Ma had spent about five years piecing together. Her hope chest stood next to it. Pa had started muttering lately about maybe its being time to start building a hope chest for me as well.

After the first window on the door side of the house was Ma's pie safe, then the door, then my jelly cupboard, wedged in between the second window and the edge of the big brick chimney. On the far side of the chimney was the dry sink, underneath the last window, and next to that, Charlie's little rope bed and the ladder up to the loft. Underneath and behind the ladder, Ma's step-back cabinet was tucked, its shelves covered with the blue-and-white salt-glazed bowls, pitchers, and plates we used each day. The blue-and-white checked curtains that we'd just barely finished hanging from the windows kind of pulled it all together and made it right homey. Pa had finally gotten around to putting a plank floor over the dirt last winter, and the colorful oval rugs Ma and I had crocheted out of rags didn't hurt, either. It seemed as though I was seeing it all for the first time. Even the boys' toys scattered about underfoot were pleasing. All this time Johnny was looking with me, then he walked over to the mantel.

"See you got a clock, Meg."

"That's Pa's pride. An eight-day clock it is, too. He winds it every Sunday night since we got it in Locust Grove, in honor of his bumper crop. 'Course he doesn't put it quite that way. Says it's to remind us of our mortality. I do admire the picture of the little village on the door, and the way its top points up sort of like a church steeple. Looks real nice sitting up there between Ma's two big pewter platters and the candlesticks."

"It does for sure." He walked carefully around the rocking chair where his father was now peacefully dozing, empty cider mug in hand. "May I admire your jelly cupboard?"

He fondled the softly gleaming maple wood that Pa had chosen for it, then opened the doors. Inside, the shelves were filled with little glazed clay pots of my preserves.

"You've been busy."

"Well, the bottom dozen or so are empty, waiting for next spring. But the others are full." I carefully pointed out the rows of strawberry, blackberry and raspberry preserves. "And here, these are apple jelly. Maybe next year we'll have some peach. Pa traded some apple saplings from the orchard with the Millers this year for some of their peach and apricot saplings. Might get a few come next summer. And here," I pointed out a bigger, rather sticky pot. "Goodness," I sighed. "The boys have been into the honey pot again. We found a honey tree last time I took Abe and Aaron fishing in early September.''

"Fish still running as good?''

"Pretty near. We've got a whole barrel full of smoked fish out in the barn for the winter. Turned out tasty. Have to give you some while you're here.''

Ma had been kind of listening this whole time while she sliced into a new ham for the supper. "If you're finished braggin' about our earthly goods, Maggie, you can get some red-eye gravy together for this ham, then whip up a batch of biscuits for the oven.''

I grinned, then took some of the fat from the ham slices and started to sizzle it in a big pan over the fire. When that was ready, I threw in the slices and browned them up some. Then I took the meat out of the pan and poured a little water and coffee from the tin coffeepot that always sat near the fire into the drippings and mixed it around a little. Ma already had the biscuits started and soon they were in the oven. Charlie was hungry and beginning to beg for food.

"Guess you can go get your Pa and the boys from the barn, Maggie.''

Johnny slipped into his boots and came with me, slamming the cabin door behind us. Pa had finished the evening milking, and he and the boys were admiring our sleek young steer.

Pa nodded hello to Johnny like it was just yesterday he'd seen him last. "What do you think, boy? Looks about ready for the slaughter to me.''

"Handsome animal, sir. I'd admire a good steak from him.''

Pa laughed. "So would we all. If the weather's fine tomorrow, maybe we'll try and get it.''

"Supper's ready, Pa.''

"So.'' He got off his knees and followed us out the barn door. There he stopped to investigate the already dark sky. "Looks like we got an early winter coming on. Way below freezing just in the last hour, and I can smell snow. Gonna be hard traveling for you and your pa, boy. Maybe you'd better put your Mabel in one of the empty stalls for the night." Then he strode into the house.

We took care of Mabel, then went in to eat. I noticed Ma had boiled up some carrots and the last of the fresh greens. They were sitting in a bowl, with butter melting out in little puddles from the spoonful on top. Old Mr. Stuart seemed in better shape and I could almost see him lick his chops at the spread in front of him while we waited for Pa to finish the praying.

When we finally started in, he had some trouble masticating the ham, but made up for it in biscuits covered with fresh butter and honey. I watched him, my own food hardly tasted, till he stopped for a moment and let out a sigh.

"Mrs. McDonald, I can truly say that you are the finest cook this side of Philadelphia. Just looking at this food brings back my old strength."

Ma beamed. "Got a hen getting on too old to lay. I'll just put her into a pot for soup tomorrow. Be easier for you than the ham."

He looked upset. "Please, madam, do not sacrifice the hen just for me."

"Nonsense, Mr. Stuart. Just waitin' for an occasion, I was. The leeks are ready, and I can make some cock-a-leeky soup."

A look of pure bliss crossed the old man's face. "Can't say how long since I had a good cock-a-leeky in front of me. It will be a pleasure, I'm sure." He reached for another biscuit. "And what transpired with your ice harvesting, Mr. McDonald?"

"Be happy to show you the icehouse in the morning, sir. Harvesting went right well, and we still have a few pieces from last winter a-lying there."

Abe spoke up then. "You were right about the ice

51

cream, Johnny. Fixed some with Maggie's berries this summer and it was past delicious.''

"You bet, Johnny," Aaron piped in, "and Maggie's teaching us how to read. Soon's we're good enough, Pa's gonna let us help with the Bible readings." He looked inordinately proud of this prospect.

Old Mr. Stuart looked at Pa. "So, my good sir, you no longer begrudge us the bringing of words to your daughter?"

Pa looked a little uncomfortable at having to make an outright confession of his change of mind. Wasn't often that Pa actually changed his mind on a subject. He speared another piece of ham and carefully covered it with my gravy, giving him extra time to phrase his words. "Well," he said carefully, "altogether your books don't seem to have done Maggie much harm. . . ."

"Not even *Rob Roy*," grinned Johnny a mite mischievously.

"Kept that'un to herself, she has. Don't see no obvious ill effects.''

"Ah, then perhaps you'd be willing to go another step and look over a very fine history of Scotland in two volumes that I happen to have picked up," voiced Mr. Stuart. "By the selfsame Sir Walter Scott. A fine addition to your daughter's education, and your sons' as well.''

"Well. . . ."

"No hurry, sir. Just remember the words from Ecclesiastes: 'Let us now sing the praises of famous men, the heroes of our nation's history.' The Good Book's all about the history of the chosen people, so I calculate God's got an interest in what's happened since to his people. Then, of course, Scotland's had a fair impact on our new country as well. . . ." He slowed down then, to let that sink in some. Then he looked at Pa, hopeful-like. " I trust we'll have a day or two of grace to stay with you whilst you think upon it.''

''Could use another pair of hands for the steer slaughtering, if your son be willing.'' Pa looked at Johnny.

''Be glad to oblige, sir.'' Then he looked at his father and back again to my Pa. ''Might I bring in Pa's pallet to put by the fire for the night? His bones are getting a mite stiff with the weather coming cold like it is. . . .''

''Of course, of course.'' Pa was feeling expansive again. ''Now when you next come, I hope to have the new rooms to the house built. Be even more comfortable for you then. Been thinking about tacking on two stories from the rear of the cabin—there where the big bed is.'' We all looked over in that direction. ''Been having a little trouble working out the layout of a staircase for the second floor, though. Would like to have one big room on the ground floor for Ma and me, and two bedrooms on the second—one for Maggie and one for the boys.''

This was the first I'd heard of a special room just for me, and I must say it whetted my interest in the proceedings considerable. ''You mean I could have my very own room just like Hildy Miller?''

''That's my thinking.''

''With a real bed and a window even?''

Pa smiled. ''Maybe *two* windows. You're getting to be a young lady now. Time for a little privacy.''

I let out a very unladylike whoop of joy.

Pa looked pleased, but said, ''That'll be enough of that, Maggie, or I'll think it's a young squaw I've got for a daughter.''

I calmed down some then and set into thinking. ''Ever see the inside of the Stuarts' wagon, Pa?'' Not waiting for an answer, I launched ahead. ''Bunk beds like they've got would be perfect for the boys' room. Takes up less space and is kind of adventuresome, too." I could see Abe and Aaron take on an immediate interest in the conversation. Even Charlie was trying to follow it some.

"Could we look at their wagon and see, Pa, please?" from the older of the two.

"Well, I'd say that was up to the Stuarts."

Johnny spoke up then. "You boys can come out with me after dinner and help to haul in Pa's pallet. Give you a good look then."

"Bring in a bit of paper and my pen and ink, too, Johnny," spoke up Mr. Stuart. "I've seen enough stairs on my travels. Seems to me I could sketch out a few ideas for Mr. McDonald."

"Thank you for the thought, sir," said Pa. "I'm more than willing to take some advice when the subject's not my own." Pa looked across the table then, and seeing that it was pretty near clean of all edibles, called for his Bible. Aaron went to get it from the Bible box atop Ma's hope chest, with Charlie trying to help, but mostly getting in the way, like youngsters his age do. Pa opened right up to the parable about the two men building their houses, one upon the sands, and the other upon solid rock. Pa had a real knack for homing right in on the most appropriate of the Lord's words for the occasion at hand.

When the book was put away again, the boys all hightailed it out to the wagon, even little Charlie. Pa went out to make his final check on the animals. I helped to clean up from the meal. Old Mr. Stuart was settled into the rocking chair for the duration. I was mighty glad Ma had thought to make some cushions for its seat and back from the last of the curtain material. I'd stuffed it up with feathers from our geese myself, and was pleased to see his old bones look so comfortable in it.

When the menfolk finally trailed back in, they were covered with snow. Ma looked a bit surprised, and I followed her to the door to look out. It was coming down fast and furious. Finally Pa appeared and slammed the door for the night.

"I'd say we got us an early blizzard coming on. Might as well get everyone tucked up for the night." He gave me a look. "There'll be no reading out in the wagon this night, Maggie."

How he could read my mind like that, I'll never know, but it sure put a cast on my high spirits.

He looked at me again. "If you two will not be disturbing Mr. Stuart too much, maybe you can whisper some by the fire."

"I assure you, sir," spoke up old Mr. Stuart, "once my body becomes vertical, I'll be disturbed by nothing."

"All right, then." Pa handed me the fat lamp from the table. "Might as well use this then, too, if you're set on reading with young Johnny. No point in ruining your eyes completely."

"Thank you, Pa!"

Ma chased the boys up the ladder, saying Charlie could sleep there tonight as a treat, and Johnny and I helped to make his Pa comfortable. Pa was already under the quilt and Ma soon to follow. Johnny gave me a wink and pulled a book out from under his shirt. I sighed with pleasure, wondering what he'd picked. Was sure to be something exciting. We curled up by the fire, and he started in telling me about this new English writer he'd recently discovered, name of Charles Dickens. And, oh, my, *Rob Roy* could hardly hold a candle to *Oliver Twist*.

We must've been at it some hours, with only the background sounds of the sleeping house and the silently falling snow, taking it in turns to read a page or two in whispers, each to the other. Young Oliver's trials in the workhouse were too much for me and, when my tears started to fall on the words and began to blur the print, Johnny closed the book.

"I think that will do for tonight, Meg," he said

softly. "You have got a gentle heart, for sure." He looked in my eyes then, and squeezed my arm. I felt a rush of warmth for him, but just wiped my eyes on my shawl and made my way up to bed.

I woke up late the next morning to a strange silence and an unexpected coldness around me. I snuggled further under my feather-tick, then peeked out to check on the boys. They were already up and gone.

I lay there for a few moments, gazing up in the dim light at the bunches of dried herbs hanging from the rafters, at the large, airy basket that held the ticks in the summer so's the down wouldn't get musty. Finally my eyes made out the pear-shaped goose-down basket that held our loose feathers beneath its narrow, lidded neck, so the feathers could breathe without escaping. Sure did make a mess when they were let loose, accidental-like. Tipped over once when the boys were wrestling one night. Thought we'd all choke for a while. Put me in mind of a bit of nonsense my Ma used to tickle the little ones with:

Goosey, goosey gander.
Where you going yonder?
"Down to the farm lot
and far as I can wander."

Then I remembered Johnny and the snow. A bit regretfully I edged out of the warmth and into my wool dress and shawl, then climbed downstairs. The place was empty except for old Mr. Stuart, dozing in the rocking chair by the fire, one of Ma's comforters tucked around his thin body. I peeked in the porridge pot. Ah! Ma had made cornmeal mush for a change.

I helped myself liberally, then doused my bowl with molasses. After my stomach felt considerably fuller and warmer, I looked toward the door. Ma had dug out my winter cape and it hung there on its peg, just waiting for me. I pulled on my boots, threw the cape around my shoulders and swung open the door. A blast of cold snow shocked me. I gazed at it a minute, hardly believing that it could still be snowing. I slammed the door shut and went back in to find my woolen muffler tucked in Ma's hope chest, then went back out to trudge through the foot or so of snow that had already fallen. If Pa hadn't thought to string up the blizzard rope between the cabin and the barn, I do believe I would've gotten lost. It was coming down that hard.

The whole family was in the barn, hovering around the carcass of the steer that Pa had already slaughtered. I was surprised. He usually liked to do the dirty work outside, away from the other animals, so as not to upset them with the sounds and smells. They were working on the far side of the barn from the stalls, though, and I guessed he figured this snow would be lying on the ground for some days, and that big steer just eating up the winter fodder fast as he was able.

"Morning, all."

"Well, look who's decided to get up," commented Pa.

"Better take off your cape and get that big leather apron on," added Ma.

Johnny just smiled, and Charlie ran over to give me a hug or two.

Ma handed me her big red hen with its neck wrung and a bucket of hot water she must've just brought out from the house before my waking. "You pluck and clean her, Maggie, so I can give your Pa and the boys a hand with the steer."

"Yes, ma'am."

Wasn't anything to do but hunker down and get on with it. Not my favorite job by a long shot. Cats loved it, though. Soon had all three of them begging 'round my legs for the warm innards. Guessed they deserved a treat now and again. I kept one eye on the other proceedings.

Pa and Johnny had rigged up some tackle and rope to pull the dead steer off the floor and now were getting on with the stripping and cutting. Right messy. Before I knew it, though, it was practically dinner-time. Ma was busy, so I took up the hen and a bucket full of fresh beef pluck—the stomach, liver, heart, and lights—and headed back into the cabin. Old Mr. Stuart was up and settled at one end of the big table, a-drawing away. I edged up to take a look after I'd pulled off my outer clothes. He had bits of paper covered with neat little sketches of rooms.

"What's all that?" I ventured.

"Just designing some options for your father's additions to the family manse."

"Oh." I looked at them carefully. "First time I've ever seen drawings of a house like that, with one wall missing. Kind of like a skeleton."

"You have a rare, original way of looking at things, Meg. Anyone ever told you that?"

"No, sir."

"Would love to leave some more books with you. A dictionary, for instance. But your father might protest vehemently."

"What's a dictionary?"

He smiled a now toothless smile. "A book full of words—and their definitions—meanings, that is."

I thought about that for a moment. "Could be rare useful. Some of those words in *Rob Roy* I never could figure out, and nobody to ask, either."

"Precisely what Mr. Webster had in mind when he compiled his fine tome."

I was about to ask what a "tome" was, then thought better of it. "Well, I'd best be getting on with the meal."

I slung the hen in a big cauldron and filled it with water and vegetables to simmer, then started in to make haggis. I cleaned the stomach bag, scalded it, scraped it, and put in to soak in cold water. Then I put

58

the other organs on to parboil. Later on, I'd chop them, add some oatmeal and suet, and a few onions from the root cellar, and stuff the mixture into the stomach. After steaming it for a few hours, and letting it cool, it could be sliced and fried for breakfast. When the cock-a-leeky was nearly ready, I set up the table for eating around Mr. Stuart, then dashed out to ring the dinner bell.

Didn't take long for everybody to come running in. They all lined up by the wash basin to clean up some of the animal gore, then stood around the fireplace toasting their fingers and kind of cluttering up my final dinner preparations. Finally had to tell them all to sit down out of the way and let me get on with the serving. Ma laughed at the thought of my serving her for a change, but let me do it. The hot, pungent soup was welcomed by the chilly family and Johnny—and old Mr. Stuart's lack of teeth didn't slow down his intake. He looked properly appreciative.

Not much talking went on, since everyone was all fired up to go back out and finish up with the slaughtering. Ma stayed to clean up after the meal and put Charlie down for a nap, and there was still a lot to do to the haggis. Hated to leave Johnny out there in the barn all afternoon, but he was busy helping Pa to saw up the meat, and I could see that he was doing a good job of it. Johnny's pa was wide awake in the rocking chair, asking Ma questions about the haggis making. He asked me if I'd mind going out to the wagon and haul in something for him. Some kind of instrument under his bunk. I did as he asked and came back with a strange boxy-looking thing.

"What is it?" I wanted to know.

"Never seen a concertina?"

"Nope."

"Well, now, it works like this." He loosened up a couple of clasps and the whole thing kind of swung open, like a bellows. There was a little keyboard on one side, with tiny ivory buttons that put me in mind of the piano I'd seen at the Millers'. He set in to squeezing the thing and out came the most remarkable music! 'Course that was the end of Charlie's nap, but Ma didn't seem to mind much. She livened up considerable and I never saw haggis making go so fast as it did that afternoon with the concertina playing and Charlie dancing around it and us in a delirium of pleasure. Ma even broke out into song a couple of times. She had a pleasing voice that I'd never heard before except during hymn singing at camp meeting. Between the two of them they taught me a few songs, too.

Mr. Stuart said they were old Scots songs, like "My Bonnie Lies Over the Ocean," and "You Take the High Road," and were composed to honor all them that left Scotland's shores after The Forty-five, never to return. Seemed sad to me never to be able to go home again, but the songs were real nice.

Johnny caught us at it when he brought in the huge steak to fry up for dinner. He was plumb filthy, but delighted when he saw what was going on, and joined in for a few rounds. Then Ma suggested, ever so gently, that perhaps we'd better be putting the music aside before Pa came in. We were all loath to do it, but could see the wisdom of it. Pa always looked for the sin attached to a little fun, and I sure didn't want to spoil the memory of that afternoon. I started in to fry the meat, and Johnny slipped back out to the wagon with his father's concertina.

That night after supper, Pa sat down next to old Mr. Stuart and went over all of his "architectural drawings," as he called them. I had to keep water boiling to give all the boys a bath in Ma's washtub. They were that filthy. Then it was Pa's turn, though he complained fiercely about having to peel off his long johns so early in the season, and it not even proper winter yet. Ma had hung a blanket from the ceiling to give him some privacy. Then she and Johnny had their turns, too. Johnny'd had to run out to the wagon again to get his fresh set of clothes and I figured Ma and I would have to wash tomorrow, snow or no snow, 'cause the pile of dirty clothes by the door was enough to scare a skunk away.

Seemed to take forever to get everyone bunked down, but we finally did it, and then Johnny and I had another go at *Oliver Twist*. Only a couple chapters, though, 'cause Johnny's head kept nodding till I was afraid it might fall off. A great pity it was, too, for we'd just come to the part about Oliver's going to live with Fagin, who looked to be the most interesting character I'd ever met, in or out of a book. More than a little wistfully I closed up the book, banked the fire, rolled Johnny far enough away from it so's he wouldn't get lit up during the night, then took myself up to the loft.

When I woke, the snow had finally stopped. But there was so much of it I knew that Johnny and his pa weren't going anywhere for a while. That made me feel better, and I didn't really mind when it came time to shove the table to one side to make room for the messy clothes-washing chore.

Johnny plowed through the snow, putting up the wash rope and, when I finally got outside with a basket full of dripping wet clothes, the sun was shining fit to burst and I could see the big piles of snow starting to melt down. He helped me hang up the clothes, then ran to the barn and came out hauling the big sled Pa had built for the boys last winter.

Johnny took me for the first ride, past the well, down the slope at the front of the house and clear to the bend in the road. By the time we tramped back with the sled in tow, Abe, Aaron, and even little Charlie were jumping around, yelling for their turns. I guess I kind of got into the spirit of things, because before any of us knew it, Ma was ringing the dinner bell and I realized I'd gotten off scot-free with the rest of my morning chores. Felt more than a little guilty going into the cabin and remembering, but Ma just gave me a big smile and said, "My, don't you all look bright and healthy!" Funny how Ma's so different from Pa in some ways.

After the meal we all helped old Mr. Stuart shuffle out to inspect the ice house, now packed full of beef. Pa had heaped a whole lot of snow on top and hoped it would hold till the real ice was ready on the lake. And just to hedge his bets, he had the smokehouse fire going, working on smoking up maybe a third of the big beast that he'd saved from freezing. After that exercise the old man was tuckered out, so he and Charlie had their naps.

Johnny took me back outside and taught me how to build a snowman. There was just no end to the things that boy could think up to do. Even had a snowball fight with me and Aaron against Johnny and Abe. Johnny said it was fairer that way. Well, Pa had been watching all this off and on with a strange expression on his face, and finally yelled for us to come and see to the animals.

It went on like that for another two days, but finally the snow melted enough for the Stuarts to harness up Mabel again and be on their way. Pa bought the *History of Scotland* and old Mr. Stuart, looking considerably spryer than when he'd arrived, insisted that Pa take a gift of Mr. Webster's dictionary. Said it would be mighty useful for plumbing the depths of the odd word or two in the Bible that Pa might've had occasion to wonder about. I remember thinking that I would've rather had *Oliver Twist*, even though Johnny and I had just managed to get through it. But I wasn't about to look a gift horse in the mouth, as some folks say. We all waved them 'round the bend, and I felt sadder than usual at the parting. Least I'd sent them off with clean clothes, darned socks, and several pots of my best preserves. Guessed you couldn't ask much more of a thirteen-year-old girl. I sure had a powerful itch to grow up.

CHAPTER 5

I WAS SITTING IN THE SWING on the new porch, with Abe and Aaron on either side of me going over their lessons in *McGuffey's Reader*. We'd finished supper and it was a hot, lazy July evening.

Pa was upstairs in the boys' new room, banging away at their bunk beds. Said maybe they'd get to sleep in them for the first time tonight. Ma was busy finishing the stuffing and sewing up of their new mattresses. With all the excitement the boys weren't paying me as much heed as usual. Can't say that I blamed them much. I'd felt pretty much the same way last week when Pa finished up my room.

And wasn't it just something! Two windows and a neat rope bed and the new hope chest Pa had cobbled together for me over the winter *and* a lovely little shelf for my books, my little Bible Pa had bought me after I got baptized, and other treasures, like the fancy cornhusk dolls I'd been making over the years. Ma had even promised me some curtain material for the windows next trip to Locust Grove. Hoped they had something nice and flowery, with maybe some pink and red and green in it. And I could hardly wait for the cool weather to set in so I could test my very own fireplace that Pa had built into the corner.

So there we were, working through Lesson Forty-one in the second reader, the story about, "One cold, bleak night, the snow fell fast, and the wind blew loud and shrill." Seemed a little out of place on this summer night. Aaron was just starting in to slowly puzzle out, "These good men sent out a dog, to hunt for those who might want help" when we heard a hound a-baying for all it was worth.

We all three looked up, mighty surprised, in the direction of the baying. Seemed to be down the road past the bend. Came nearer then, followed by the sounds of a horse and wagon. My heart dropped. Couldn't be Johnny. He never did have a dog. Neither did we, for that matter. Just never seemed to collect one. I put down the book and we all got off that swing so fast it nearly clipped me a good one.

Sure was a dog and here it came. Running fast toward us. Seemed to be a good-looking bitch with nice liver markings. Finally screeched to a halt before us, panting up a storm, long ears flopping and tail a-wagging. We stared at the mysterious creature a moment, ignoring the wagon closing in behind.

It was Charlie, come out of the cabin from helping Ma to see what the ruckus was who let out the yell, "Johnny's wagon!"

I looked up slowly, trying to be casual-like. That hound just climbed up the porch steps and settled down like she owned the place. I grinned at her a moment, then bounded after the boys to welcome our friends back. Johnny's pa was sitting up on the wagon board next to Johnny, looking spry as ever I'd seen him. Still, he did creak a bit as Johnny lowered him to the ground. The whole family was out back now, and old Mr. Stuart made one of his best sweeping bows.

"The Stuarts, father and son, have returned. And

we are still the best purveyors of books, inspirational and educational, moralistic and fanciful, in the states of Pennsylvania, Ohio, and beyond.''

Even Pa cut a smile.

Ma was all lit up, then looked a little worried. ''But you've come too late for supper!'' She thought a moment, then, ''Still, there's a good hunk of cherry pie left. Wouldn't go down bad with some cool milk.''

''Madam,'' started in old Mr. Stuart, ''of the million-odd residents of this state, there's no one's pie I'd rather eat.'' Ma blushed right pretty, and Johnny's pa took the time to admire our new addition to the house. Clapboards were only up on the front side yet, but it looked right pretty. ''I can see that sloth will never be a resident in this household, sir. You must've started in on the building directly after we left last year.''

Pa looked pleased as punch. ''Near to, after the first snows melted. Your sketches got me going real good. But come now, set yourself on the porch. Ma and I been waitin' on company to test the new swing. Maggie and the boys have near taken it over as their own.''

We helped him up onto the porch and settled him into the swing, then I ran inside to get the pie and fixings. Soon we were all setting around the porch on that lovely night, even the hound in a state of delight with a bone I'd given it.

''Well, Johnny,'' I finally looked at him, ''where'd you get the dog?''

He looked back at me. He wasn't that much taller, but he'd filled out considerable, and from the cast of his face in the light of the almost full moon, I could see that he'd be shaving in earnest now. He let out a deep, rich laugh. Voice had thickened up some, too.

''Felicity adopted us not long after we pulled out of here last fall. Found her near the side of the road with a broken leg. Must've got caught in a trap and pulled herself out. I set the leg and she recuperated inside the wagon with Pa. Pa pointed out that it was mighty felicitous having a combination companion and leg-warmer, so we just took to calling her 'Felicity'."

Knowing we were talking about her, Felicity put aside her bone, stood up on her short legs and shook herself some.

"Looks like mighty good hunting stock, there," commented Pa.

"It's possible, sir, possible," commented old Mr. Stuart. "But I doubt she'll ever have the need with us. She adapted to home life very quickly. Possibly too quickly." He looked at Johnny. "Best haul out the basket, son."

"Yes, Pa."

Johnny headed off to the wagon and we all eyed him, wondering what could be in the basket. He returned to plunk down a basket full of puppies, and we all let out a roar of laughter. The boys and I crowded around the puppies. There were three of them, about four weeks old.

"Looks like you got more than you bargained for with Felicity, Johnny."

"Guess so," he smiled. "They're just about ready to be broken from their Ma and sure could use a good home."

We all turned to look at Pa then, all except for Charlie, who'd picked up one of the pups and was hugging it to him, love spreading out all over his face.

"Please, Pa. This one is mine." The pup licked Charlie's nose, then peed all over him in a fit of excitement.

"Sure seems to have made his mark on Charlie," I commented, and we all laughed.

I could see Ma give Pa a little look. "Can't see how it could be a harm, Jamie. The boy could use something young like the pup for company."

"Well. . . ." Pa was scratching his ear.

We all waited, kind of holding our breaths.

"Well, maybe so."

"Oh, *thank you*, Pa," whispered Charlie.

'Course then Abe and Aaron wanted the other two. Never heard such a ruckus going on. Finally Felicity took over, herded the pups together and settled down to nurse them. Pa finally said we'd wait a day on deciding about the other two while Johnny and his father rested up some. We'd have to see how the pups took to the place. Pa decided it was past time for the boys to be in bed, so of course we all had to march up the new stairs, lugging the mattresses, admiring Pa's handiwork by candlelight. Even had a peek at my room before wishing the boys good night.

Took another little while to settle down old Mr. Stuart and say good night to Ma and Pa. Then Johnny and I were out on the porch, just swinging, peaceful-like. He kind of edged out his hand and took mine in his, and it felt ever so natural and right there. Didn't even think to inquire about any good new books to read. Guess we could have set there for a fair spell if Pa hadn't suddenly pounded on the wall from his new bedroom and yelled out, "Get to bed, Maggie!"

"Yes, Pa!" I swan, that man never could have been fourteen-and-a-half years old on a hot summer's night!

Come morning, I bolted out of bed with the first rays of light through my windows. It'd been a whole week, but I still couldn't get used to seeing all that light come poking in. Guessed it would take awhile to forget the dark loft. Kind of missed the smells of herbs floating in the air, too, and the funny old loft ladder. But the new staircase was certainly fine, and I bounced down it with a whistle on my lips.

Ma was already up, starting in to knead the bread dough. I gave her a hand with that, then went out to milk the cow. When I got back, Ma decided some fresh butter would be nice, so I filled up the churn and started in to pound it. Just about then I heard someone working the well. I looked out the window and watched Johnny get set to strip off his shirt for a wash. Guessed I would have just stood there admiring his fine back if Ma hadn't caught on and given me a poke.

"You're gettin' to the age where a little privacy is to be respected, Maggie."

"Yes, ma'am. But why? Practically been watching Johnny grow up for the past five years. Seems to me he's nearly family."

"Nearly, but not quite." And Ma set a few loaves into the oven, the subject obviously closed. I just sighed. Sure was a funny age when you were almost grown up, but not quite. Never got a straight answer. Have to be taking some questions to Hildy Miller come October.

Just then, all my brothers came barrelling down the new stairs. Hadn't expected them up just yet. Sure couldn't have got much sleep last night. They had been bouncing around, arguing about who got to sleep in the top bunk when I fell asleep last night. I dished up their porridge, then sat down with some myself. Needn't have bothered if it was the company I was looking for. They were through that porridge and out the door faster'n a cat after a treed possum. I looked at Ma.

She smiled. "Guess they're excited about the puppies."

"Guess so." I set about trying to look glum, something I'd been toying with recently, but then Johnny came in and I forgot all about it. Ma gave him his breakfast and he launched into it, coming up for air to ask how my reading was going.

I slowly cleaned out my bowl. "Read the *History of Scotland* twice, and been through Webster's three times now, cover to cover. And I've been reading a chapter a day from my Bible. Guess I'm looking for something to try out my new *vocabulary*."

He grinned. "How about I help you with the chores, then open up the wagon's bookshelf for you. Give you a chance to pick for yourself for a change."

"Johnny! Would you?"

"Don't see why not. Maybe we can find something to tempt your Pa with, as well."

"Just watch how you use the word *temptation*, please, Johnny. 'Specially in front of Pa. Sets him off, it does, and I'm here thinking how we'll convince him to let us whip up some ice cream tonight."

"Well, seeing as how it's likely to be hotter than a desert today, I for one don't plan to tempt your father's ire. Could do with some ice cream."

Ma stood by listening. "You youngsters better clear out before Pa gets back in for his breakfast and starts in hearing your talk. Likely to throw all the books out of the house, he is, and *The Indian Physician* just got me through Charlie's measles this spring." We grinned and left.

After we'd finished with the chickens and set Mabel out to graze in the pasture with the cow, I pointed out some of Pa's new farm innovations to Johnny. I waved out toward the west where the forest was diminishing under Pa's cutting and burning.

"Cleared another ten acres or so this winter, even with the house building. If he keeps at it, he'll be clear up to the lake soon."

"Must be getting a good price for his grain."

"Yup. Wheat's up from forty cents to two dollars a bushel now, and corn to six bits. Pa can get fifty or sixty bushels of corn to the acre, too, especially now that he's got Gibbs' improved plow. He's seriously thinking of investing in one of McCormick's new reapers this fall if the harvest's good as usual. Says with a spread of more than a hundred acres, it's plumb justified."

Johnny chuckled.

"What's so funny?"

"Just enjoying the thought of your Pa's working with his new toys."

"Johnny! They're not toys. They're *equipment*."

He chuckled some more. "I sure am admiring your new words, too. And I do like your hair that way, down your back in the big braid. Bet it's lovely combed out with the sun shining on it."

"Johnny Stuart!" And I started running back toward the house. He caught up with me soon enough, and, laughing, led me to the books in his wagon. He hopped up and, with a flourish, let down the side. We both stood there admiring the books.

"Go ahead. You can touch them."

"Really?" I reached over and pulled out the closest to me, a slim pamphlet titled *Burke's Speech on the Conciliation of the Colonies*.

"That's political stuff. Sold one to the Millers a few days back.

"Same Millers that we stay with? You know them?"

"Sure. Hildy said to say hello to you."

"You know Hildy Miller?" I wailed, visions of her gleaming blond hair and pert looks washing over me.

"Why not? Guess we know just about everybody in the state, outside of the cities." He gave me a sharp look. "Here, now. Bet you didn't know that Hildy's got a sweetheart."

I shoved back the Burke pamphlet, suddenly agog to hear the gossip. "No! Do tell!"

Johnny grinned. "A young German farmer who picked up a piece of land on the other side of their place has been coming a-courting. Name of Bernd Zimmerman. Only been in the new country a few years and mostly speaks the German. Hildy can understand it, though. Makes it harder to sell books to him, of course, but we did manage to talk him into a copy of the *New England Primer*."

"But what about Hildy?" I asked, breathlessly. "Is she interested? She's only a few months older than I, but I guess that'd make her fifteen."

"Don't really know Hildy's mind, but she did blush some when Zimmerman's name came up. Heard her Pa say, though, that she had to wait until she was sixteen afore she made up her mind."

I drew in my breath. Sixteen. Was that the magic age? Then my eyes were drawn back to the books. Since I had a ways to go anyhow, might as well get back to earth. My eyes slowly glided over the bindings, stopping to decipher titles and authors' names. A lot of Bible tracts, some agricultural works, three or four copies of *The Indian Physician*. Must be a big seller, that one. Then I spotted several thick volumes with names I didn't recognize. I pulled out the first. "William Shakespeare," I read aloud. "*The Complete Plays.*"

I looked up. "What's a play?"

"It's a story written up to be acted out by real people, on a stage. Guess you've never seen one. But I have, in Philadelphia. Real fine, they are, too."

"What's a stage?"

"Golly, Meg, but you've a lot still to learn." He sounded almost exasperated.

"Teach me, Johnny!"

"All right. Let's take this Shakespeare." He thought for a minute. "Maybe we ought to do some fishing, too."

That one had me mystified, for sure. What had fishing got to do with acting plays? But I was game, so we went and got permission from Ma, collected all the gear and headed off to the lake. When we got there, Johnny carefully selected the same overhanging rocks from two summers ago, baited the lines, then put down the rods and weighted them down with a few rocks.

"What're you doing?"

"Letting the fish do the work while I do the teaching." He pulled out the Shakespeare, then stood me up. "Here. We can make believe that this big rock is a stage." He pointed toward the lake gently lapping at its sides. "The lake is the audience. At least we'll make believe that the fish swimming in it are people, listening to us perform a play for them. Now, what shall we choose?" He leafed through the volume for a moment, then grinned. "Seems like *Macbeth* would be a good one to start with. It's set in Scotland, and has a fair amount of adventure. I'll be Macbeth. You'll be Lady Macbeth, and we can take turns with the other parts."

"Wait a minute!" Something was tugging at my mind. "Would this be the same Macbeth as Scott writes about in his *History*?

"The selfsame."

"Well, now I recognize that Shakespeare name all right. Scott said as how he'd got the story from Holinshed, whoever he may be, and Shakespeare. And my, but it was an exciting one!"

"Well, Shakespeare wrote lots of those."

"Is he still alive, like Dickens?"

"Afraid not. He lived during the time of Elizabeth I of England, and a few years into the reign of James I."

"Oh." That was kind of disappointing. I sure did have a lot of years to catch up on.

"Never mind. The play's the thing!"

And so we set into it. My, but Johnny made a fearsome witch! But I got to join in on "Fair is foul, and foul is fair: Hover through the fog and filthy air."

We'd gotten clear through the first act and I was getting the hang of it when Johnny thought to stop and check the fish lines. Good thing, too, for we hauled up two nice ones, rebaited, and got on with the play.

Wasn't till Banquo's ghost appeared at Macbeth's banquet table that we thought to eat our lunch. And then I was so fired up to continue it that I could scarce swallow or pull up the next fish. Can't say we carried as many fish home as we did on our first fishing trip, but I was so excited by this Shakespeare that it didn't seem to matter.

As we trotted back across the fields near supper-time, Johnny was thinking aloud. "We did pretty well with *Macbeth* today, but I'm thinking we'll do even better with *Romeo and Juliet*."

"Who're they?"

"Two star-crossed lovers, just about our ages, who lived in Italy long before Shakespeare wrote about them."

"What's *star-crossed* mean?"

"Means it wasn't meant for them to get together and live a happily married life."

"Don't think I'll like that one much."

"Oh, but it's so tragic that you won't be able to resist, Meg."

"Not sure about that." I wasn't about to mess up my head with any tragic love stories. Had a happy ending in mind for myself, I did.

Johnny laughed. "It's only make-believe, Meg. Shakespeare was one of the world's greatest writers—ever. He meant for us to laugh and cry with his characters. He was a smart man. Knew that it helped people to look into themselves and learn. He's got some happy lovers, too, like Petruchio and Kate in *The Taming of the Shrew*."

"Well, let's do them next. Don't know that much about lovers that I can take the chance with starting off with unhappy ones."

He roared, and took my hand in his for a moment

74

and looked into my eyes. "I sure do want to be around when you finish growing up, Meg."

"Well, I plan to be here, like usual. Just see that you are, too." He came mighty close and almost brushed my face with his, and my heart skipped a few beats. 'Course Ma chose that moment to ring the supper bell and we hadn't any choice but to head on in through the shoulder-high corn.

After Ma's usual fine dinner, we all set out on the porch and Pa and Mr. Stuart started in on talking politics while the boys played with Felicity and her pups just below in the dust. Johnny and I were chopping up ice to put in a wooden bucket that Pa had fixed up with a lid and moveable handle, kind of like a small butter churn. We listened in and pounded away at the cream cooling inside, our mouths already watering for the ice cream dessert.

"Guess you'll be voting for Harrison come election time, Mr. McDonald."

"Don't see why not, if I can get near enough to a voting poll."

"Figured as much. He is an Ohio resident, though seems to me he was born in Virginia."

"Won't hurt none to have an Ohioan in Washington. Maybe he'll address some of our problems."

"They sure are setting up a bandwagon around the country with this election. Every small town we pass through, we see free kegs of hard cider and the slogan 'Tippecanoe and Tyler, Too' set out for the voters' delectation."

"Can't say I approve of selling votes with hard cider."

"Other side's doing it, too. Guess they figure there's a lot of hard cider drinkers out there."

"Not gonna get 'em the church voters, once they find out. Kind of puts my mind in a different perspective on the subject, it does."

"Maybe not. Still, Harrison's an old war horse, all right. Saw in the *Cincinnati Daily Gazette* where it might've been better to run Henry Clay for the Whigs, though. Would've put a damper on this slavery business some. As it stands now, Harrison and the Whig party have avoided stating any political views on anything. Didn't even adopt a platform at their convention, just slogans. Like the 'Tippecanoe' one, and 'Harrison, Two Dollars a Day, and Roast Beef.' Now I ask you, sir, what is our fine country coming to?''

Well, I kind of lost interest at that point, since the ice cream was starting to come up nice and smooth. I ran inside for some bowls and spoons and soon even the puppies were cast aside for the treat. 'Course, Charlie did try to spoonfeed some to his pup. Called him "Dog," so I guessed that was the name that would stick. Abe and Aaron had a higher level of sensibilities already. Abe was calling his 'Rab' after the dog in his *McGuffey's Primer*, and Aaron had settled on 'Nell' for his little bitch from the same source. Nice to see them starting to take some notice to their education.

Even Pa seemed to be enjoying the ice cream. I'd thrown in near a whole jar of my best strawberry preserves for flavoring, and I must say it was the tastiest ever. Then it was time to retire. The boys didn't set up too much of a fuss. Guess they planned on doing some more bouncing in their new room.

I begged Pa to let Johnny and me have a lantern out on the porch for some reading, seeing as how they planned to set off bright and early the next morning. First he said no, but after a look from Ma he relented. Johnny said maybe Shakespeare would keep people awake, but he knew of another yarn I'd like and ran out to the wagon to find it. Turned out to be *Robinson Crusoe* by Daniel Defoe. I liked it just fine.

And the next morning, old Mr. Stuart actually got

Pa talked into buying it. Said as how it was a fine story of resourcefulness in the face of disaster, and had many moral and physical characteristics to teach the boys. Even was based on the true adventures of a real Scots sailor, one Alexander Selkirk. That was all right by me, 'cause from the first fifty pages or so, it looked to be one whopper of a tale.

After Mabel was harnessed up and old Mr. Stuart sitting in splendor in front of the wagon, Johnny took me aside and apologized for not being able to leave me with their only volume of Shakespeare, since it had been promised last season to a farmer on their way back through Pennsylvania. To make up for it, he slipped me a copy of Sir Walter Scott's *Ivanhoe*. Said it was about the days of knights in shining armor and I'd be sure to admire it.

Also said we'd carry on with *Romeo and Juliet* the next visit, that he figured I'd be ready for it by then. He pressed my hand, and touched my face softly when nobody was looking. Then he was off.

I moped around the place for nearly a week after that till Ma gave me a fine talking-to and I pulled myself together some.

CHAPTER 6

IT WAS MIDSUMMER of the next year and I was out collecting herbs to be dried for Ma's home remedies. Ma always called midsummer the "balmy time." Guess she just naturally connected it with the picking of the healing herbs, like balm or balsam. We always did it this time of year when the plants were mature and had their greatest vigor.

God had provided a nice dry, sunny day, and I hadn't started in too early, on account of dewy flowers and stems seemed to just fall apart after awhile and lose all their strength. I took care not to bruise the flowers or leaves, either, but gently placed them in my knapsack soon's I picked them.

It wasn't more than ten in the morning, but already I'd traveled a fair distance from the house. Didn't want to use up all the wild things in one spot—didn't seem that would be good stewardship—so I just chose a few choice samples from a patch, then moved along. It was pleasantly warm in the sun and I got to thinking about getting the plants back to the loft and spreading them out in the dark, one by one, to dry properly. Had to remember to go up and turn them each day, too. Didn't want them to rot on me. Finally figured I had enough for the first trip and set off back to the house. Could've knocked me over with a straw when I saw old Mr. Stuart sitting on the porch, and Johnny busy watering Mabel. I nodded to Johnny, ladylike, having a hard time keeping back the huge grin I felt busting out all over, then walked up to pay my respects to his father. He doffed his mangy old hat.

"The young lady of the house is blossoming, I see. And what's that I smell?" He nodded toward the knapsack. "So you've been picking herbs on this fine day before the feast of St. John the Baptist."

"Yes, sir. The right time of year for it, it is. But I'm not the only young lady of the house, as you'll soon see and hear. Ma and Pa and the rest of us were blessed with little Sarah a few months back."

Ma appeared at the door with Sarah in her arms and brought her over to be admired. Old Mr. Stuart gave her a good look and patted the soft red hair on her head with his slightly shaky, bony old hand. She let out a squawk.

"Looks like you've got another young Maggie on your hands, Mrs. McDonald. She's got the fire of hair and spirit."

Ma just smiled, then said, "Guess another one like Maggie will be no hardship. She's becoming a good, Christian woman. Wouldn't mind a little less forthrightness at times, though."

Old Mr. Stuart nodded and asked if he could have a look at my herbs. Ma bustled back in to put Sarah in her cradle, and I unshouldered the pack and opened it on the swing next to him. He set right in to musing.

"Take me right back to my old mother, those smells." He poked at one. "Just look at this *geranium robertanium*. Guess that would be crane's bill to you. It's been prescribed for gastric ulcers, diarrhea, hemorrhages, and even diabetes. When I was a small child I remember seeing my mother crush the fresh leaves—foul smell they have—to keep off mosquitoes.''

"That's a new one on me," I ventured. "'Course I know about marigolds' keeping off small bugs from the garden. Always keep a border of them around the kitchen garden.''

"You refer to the *calendula officinalis*, of course. Old King Henry IV of France deplored the fact that they were so little used in medicine despite all the properties attributed to them. If you drink an infusion of them three or four times a day, they are quite helpful for hysteria, ulcers, and the women's problem. Externally used, they soothe the pain of burns. Surgeons even used them during our Revolution applied to the scalp to cure impetigo and milk-crust.''

I looked at him in wonder. "You do know a powerful lot of things, sir.''

He looked pleased. "Used to study botany a bit. Always did love to read. Take this sweet marjoram, for instance.'' He'd picked up another one of my plants and I held my breath for fear he'd crush it in his fingers, unknowing-like, with that little palsy he'd seemed to pick up since last year. Luckily he paid me no heed. "Also known as *origanum vulgar* it is. The ancient Greeks used to plant it over their tombs to give peace to the spirits of the departed. . . .''

I could tell now that he was set to go on all day on this subject. Not that I'd mind, but I could see Johnny hovering a bit behind me, a grin starting up on his face, and if I didn't get these herbs set out in the dark soon, the morning's work on them would be lost. I decided it was timely to put my cache of herbs away in the loft right then. I apologized to Mr. Stuart and scampered off the porch with my pack.

When I got back down Johnny was on the porch with Felicity, the dog lapping up a bowl of milk, and

Johnny trying my fresh-squeezed cherry juice. He looked even bigger than ever, and manly in a powerful sort of way. His eyes were still dancing under his curly black hair, though.

"Hello, Meg."

"Hello, Johnny." Seemed to have a good deal of trouble pulling my eyes away from his. Kept seeing him as Ivanhoe disguised as the disinherited knight, and I, Rowena, accepting his crown before the eyes of all at the tourney.

He must've been a mindreader, for he asked me then what I'd thought of *Ivanhoe*.

I blushed to the roots of my red hair. Must've been a fair sight, that.

"Ah." he looked at me. "I think you stand ready for more Shakespeare, Meg. Maybe even *Romeo and Juliet*."

His father smiled knowingly and Ma, who'd come out again to sit a bit, just said, "Get off with you both until dinnertime. Mr. Stuart can keep Sarah and me company."

Johnny proffered a hand to pull me off the steps and we went off to take Mabel to the pasture. We set her loose, then wandered in the field ourselves, finally sitting down under a tree next to the little gurgling stream. Pa had picked up a mare last fall at camp meeting, and she'd surprised us all by foaling this spring, a lovely little roan-colored filly with gangling legs. We watched the two cavort about the field, enjoying each other's company.

"Nice to see young things like that, this time of year," commented Johnny.

"Sure is. The boys are already arguing over who gets to train and break her. Pa bought the mare to help Blackie with the plowing, but suddenly the boys are all keen on buying saddles and riding a proper mount. Guess they'll probably have their way. Usually do with Pa."

"It's only natural. He's looking to have sons to help more and more with his farm, and take over from him eventually. Behooves him to keep them excited about the possibilities. There's a whole lot of new land out West they could be moving on to in a few years." He had that faraway look again.

"You're thinking about that 'prairie-ocean' again, Johnny. I can see it."

"And why not? It's getting a little too civilized around here. Why, just look at yourselves. Few years back, you had a small spread and a one-room cabin. Now you've got more than a hundred acres to work, and a real house—with whitewashed clapboards and shutters painted red, even."

"God has been good to us," I smiled, "but painting the shutters red was my idea. Adds a nice touch to the place. And did you notice my flower beds around the house?"

"Just what I was referring to. Civilization! Why, look, your Pa's even got a weather vane atop the barn now." He turned about some and pointed to the big iron rooster proudly perching on top of the barn roof, with its arrow underneath pointing out the wind's direction.

"Yup. Pa invested in that last fall at Locust Grove. Said it would help him some with keeping on top of sudden storms. I do believe he had one in mind, though, ever since the Millers started in bragging about theirs. And did you notice his new windmill?" I pointed to the wooden tower not far from us. "It's been a big help already in hauling up water for the crops during dry spells."

Johnny shook himself, kind of frustrated-like. "It's a thing of beauty all right to your Pa, and I admire his spirit in pursuing these niceties. But don't you see, Meg? It's all a part and parcel of this piece of wilderness being hemmed in. I've a yen to see some Indians and buffalo, take the books out to those that'll be needing them to keep away the snowed-in winter melancholy."

"But Johnny, we still get snowed in here! Though I must say, it's a lot more comfortable now. Less drafty, I mean, with those clapboards over the logs, and the inside walls plastered up so pretty. Sure keeps down the bug population, too. And we still get melancholy. Leastways, I do! You've never been out here in deep winter. You're always off to the big city with your pa."

"True enough. And spending winters with my ailing pa in a cold city boarding house ain't my idea of how to spend the rest of my life. Got to break loose sometime. Don't know how I can stand many more of those city winters. You've never been there, Meg, so you just have no idea! This past year we wintered in New York City for some variety. Pa was looking for a change of scenery and maybe some good buys in old books." He leaned back against the tree trunk and ran a hand through his hair, remembering.

"Let me just tell you, Meg, there's some that thrive in the city, but I am not one of them. First off, there's the air. Smoke everywhere from the factories they're starting up. Most people just say we ought to be grateful for God's goodness in making work, which makes smoke, which makes prosperity, but I for one cannot see how God would want his good clean air fouled up so badly. Then there's all the horses on the streets. Any idea how it smells to have all the streets of a really big city clogged up with animal dung, so you hardly know where to step? And littered with uncollected garbage that brings on the rats and sickness? They've got a running joke up there about travelers entering the city being warned to get their smelling salts ready. I swan, Meg, it's a real disaster, and bound to get worse with all the new emigrants getting off the boats from the old world every day. I used to walk down to the harbor and watch them lugging their belongings off the ships, excitement in their eyes at the new life before them. Just hope they have enough sense to keep on traveling west. Like I hope to do soon.''

He closed his eyes a moment on visions only he could see. "For starters, I figure I could move the wintering to someplace like Cincinnati. Pigs or no, there is a library to study from in the winter and bookstores to restock the wagon. That way, I could start out a good five hundred miles further west in the spring, then head out from there. Into Indiana, Illinois, Missouri. Maybe even pick up with one of those wagon trains that organize from Independence. They get *hundreds* of families setting out on those things. Just imagine the glory of being among one of those treks, with a wagon full of books!''

I looked at him, worried some, and not only for myself.

"Not yet, Johnny. Your pa needs you.''

"Don't I know it.'' He looked at me then and reached for my hand. "Don't worry, Meg. I'm not about to leave him. He and the books are all I've got in this world. Except maybe you.''

"You've got the Lord smiling down on you, too, Johnny, and don't ever forget it. Bible says 'My God shall supply all your needs according to his riches in glory by Christ Jesus.' When the time is ripe, you'll have what you need.''

"When will the time be ripe for me to have *you*, Meg? Don't think I can bear going further west without you. I did a fair amount of looking at those city girls this winter, but all I could think about was you. They all took on red hair and freckles, but none of them had your spunk.'' He pulled me close under that tree then and there and placed a gentle kiss on my lips. I suddenly had a good idea of what Hildy Miller had been raving about last fall with her Bernd. Felt right nice and I could've returned it with no trouble at

84

all, but Ma, bless her timing, started in to ring the dinner bell.

Felicity and her pups, grown up now, were having a right nice reunion in front of the house when we went in to eat. Abe and Aaron were sitting on either side of Pa. Shooting right up, they were, and putting on more freckles and tan everyday. They'd been out in the fields with Pa and I guess they kind of looked upon themselves as practically grown up already. Still, they did cast looks of awe at Johnny's girth and bearing. Pa acknowledged Johnny's presence with a nod, then started in praying. After a glance at old Mr. Stuart's latest affliction, the palsied hands, he tacked on a postscript: "And remember the words of the Lord, 'Beloved, I wish above all things that thou mayest prosper and be in health, even as thy soul prospereth.'"

Ma had done up a nice beef roast for the company with a side dish of carrot pudding, and fruit jumbles out of dried apricots for dessert. Old Mr. Stuart did a good job on his pudding, but just spooned up a little of the meat gravy. Must be a real problem for Johnny to keep him nourished, with no teeth and all, I thought. I wondered what it was like to live in a boarding house all winter. I'd have to ask Johnny more about that.

After we finished eating, Johnny carried the rocking chair out onto the porch for his father to rest in, where he could catch some of the afternoon breezes. Charlie was kind of hanging around the old man with Dog and his wooden pig pull toy that Pa had surprised him with last Christmas. Charlie wasn't about to come right out and ask, but I figured Mr. Stuart was smart enough to see that the boy was looking for some stories. And he just kept clattering that pig on its wooden wheels back and forth on the porch till Mr. Stuart started in asking him if he knew that one about George Washington and the cherry tree.

"No, sir." The pig had fallen to the wayside,

forgotten, and Charlie was already sitting on his haunches, Indian fashion, in front of the rocking chair.

Johnny smiled at the picture before us. "Guess maybe we could disappear for some stories as well, Meg. I figure your Ma knows by this time that she'll get little use out of you during our visits."

I looked at him. "You did remember to bring the Shakespeare, like you promised?"

"Think I'd forget a promise to you, Meg? Let's go pick it up from the wagon, then head back to the pasture. Seems a pleasant enough spot for our readings, and maybe the cow will benefit from a little education."

I grinned and followed him.

Johnny was standing in the pasture near the tree with two good-sized sticks he'd picked up along the way. "Now if we're going to do this play up right, Meg, we'll have to practice a little fencing first."

"Fencing?"

" Sword-fights have always been one of my favorite parts of Shakespeare. He always threw in a bit of action to keep the groundlings happy."

"Whoever were they?"

"Well, look here." He took one of the sticks and drew me over to a small bare patch of ground near the stream, grass worn down from its being the cow's favorite spot to drink. He started in sketching in the mud. "Look here. See this circle-like shape? It's meant to be a building; in fact, The Globe, the name of Shakespeare's theater in old London. Named it that and built it like that so's people would get the idea they were really going to see and hear stories from all over the world. Shakespeare was smart. He was setting up their minds to adventure before they even bought their tickets. The poorest people always bought the cheapest tickets—that'd be on the ground in front of the stage where there were no seats—so they called them 'groundlings.' They'd bring their lunch or dinner with them as well. If there wasn't enough action on the stage, they'd just make some of their own by throwing food at the actors. That's why Shakespeare always managed to write in some good sword fights."

I looked at him in awe. He was a natural-born teacher. Could take you right back in time to the middle of things.

"Now when *Romeo and Juliet* starts, some of the local youngsters in Italy. . . ."

"Where's Italy?"

"Never mind. It's beyond England. I'll show you on an atlas when we get back to the house."

"All right."

"Anyhow, these youngsters weren't more than our age, and more than anything they liked a good fight. There were two clans in this city of Verona. . . ."

"Sort of like the Campbells and the McDonalds?"

"Exactly. But they were called the Montagues, that was Romeo's family, and the Capulets, that was Juliet's family. And these families had an old hatred behind them, just like the McDonalds and the Campbells, and the children weren't allowed to mix with each other. Trouble comes when young Romeo sets his eyes on Juliet and falls madly in love with her." He looked at me. "Think we ought to practice our swordplay a bit before we get into this thing, put us in the proper spirit."

Well, it didn't take much coaxing to get me into the proper spirit. Before you knew it, we were crashing sticks together, dancing across the pasture, scaring the livestock clear to the far side. Must've dropped my guard for a moment, for suddenly Johnny had his stick poked right in my middle, saying, "And now, varlet, you shall die!"

Laughing, I flung myself onto the ground and he

followed. We were rolling together over and over down the hill to the stream. When we stopped the laughing and caught our breaths, Johnny was so close I could see his eyes go all serious. He bent his head to my lips, and our lips touched again for a moment before he pulled himself away.

"Oh, Meg girl. How I crave those strawberry lips of yours. And I can see the oceans of the earth in your blue eyes."

"Don't forget the carrots of the soil in my hair."

"Don't be casting aspersions on your lovely hair, girl. Or the rest of you, either."

I sat up, more than a little muddled. "Maybe we'd best be getting back to the play, Johnny."

He smiled a bit ruefully. "You may be right. I'm pressing my favors before time." He helped me up and we went over to the book left under the tree where we sedately settled ourselves for the story.

Didn't take me long to get into the story, either. That Romeo sure had a way with words. And Juliet wasn't any slouch, either. I sure did take to that balcony scene, and Johnny played it up proper. He went off a way from the tree and gazed at me, misty-eyed, with his " 'But soft! what light through yonder window breaks? It is the east, and Juliet is the sun.' " To think I'd put him off a whole year on this play. And me not wanting any tragic love stories. By the time the sun was setting down towards the west, I was dying most pitifully and Romeo was giving me a final embrace. I finally woke up from the spell, lightly in Johnny's arms.

"Got a handkerchief?" I snuffled. "Can't go back to the house for supper in this state."

Johnny pulled himself away with some visible effort and pulled a clean bit of rag out of his pocket. We shared that rag, then went and washed our faces in the stream.

"Oh, my," I sighed. "That was mighty stressful, but felt strangely good."

"It's called *catharsis*, Meg."

"What?"

"Oh, nothing, just something one of the ancient Greeks came up with. He was a playwright, too, like Shakespeare. Name of Aristotle. Said a story that could bring you out of yourself into the troubles of others was good for the growing of the soul."

"Smart man, that."

Johnny gathered up the book and we slowly made our way back from Italy to a farm in Ohio.

After supper that night Johnny hauled a big old book of maps, an atlas, out of the wagon and set it alongside the volume of Shakespeare on the porch. We sat by lamplight after everyone else had gone to sleep, just chasing away the summer moths and turning through page after page of countries, him telling me about each one.

After a while I just sighed. "Had no idea there were so many places in the world. And me—never been any further than Locust Grove. Not even down to see the river."

Johnny thought a moment, then, "Why don't we try your pa out on that river idea again? Maybe if we took Abe and Aaron along, he'd consider it. Gonna be a mighty fine day for a good long walk tomorrow, by the look of the stars tonight."

"Oh, Johnny! Do you think he might say yes?" I had started in to bouncing at just the thought of it.

"Simmer down, Meg. No use in waking the whole household."

"Can't help it, Johnny. I'm just itching for adventure."

"The *Ivanhoe* kind?"

"Or even the *Robinson Crusoe* kind. We could make believe we're hacking our way through the jungle on a desert island. Only it will be ever so much nicer having you for company than just Friday." I kind of sank my head against his shoulder, dreaming. He put his arm lightly around me.

"I can go along with that. Fact is, I can go along with any kind of dreaming on midsummer night. That's why I brought the Shakespeare back up here. Thought you might enjoy a few snatches from his most fantastical play, *A Midsummer Night's Dream*. The old Europeans always thought this night was magical, and he's written up a fine play about humans mixing themselves up in the world of fairies on the one night of the year that anything can happen."

"Anything?" I whispered.

"Long as it's lovers that's involved," he answered softly.

I snuggled up right comfortably next to him then, and listened blissfully as he told the tale of Puck and Titania and poor Bottom, interjecting his story with bits and pieces of the talk from the book.

When he'd finished we just sat there under the spell of the story and the big old yellow moon that was starting to disappear over the trees. It surely was a magical night. We were both looking up at the piece of open sky, and both saw the star streak across it.

"Johnny!" I gasped. "A falling star!"

"No, Meg," he answered ever so softly. "A rising star. Ours." Then he gave me a little hug and led me to the door. Said he'd sleep out on the porch, under the stars. He whispered after me as I went in, very softly, so I almost didn't hear it, " 'Joy and fresh days of love accompany your heart!' "

I woke up still thinking about last night's mystery and magic. But I soon cast it to the back of my mind when I remembered about the possible adventure of today. Johnny and I bearded Pa at his breakfast. Guess we kind of caught him with his guard down, presenting the question like we did when he had a big fried egg halfway into his mouth. He sputtered some and almost choked, then Abe and Aaron were up from their seats, pounding his back and begging to be allowed to go along.

"Wait just one minute!" he roared. "Never promised nobody a trip to the river, leastways you boys. You were set to help me out on the north field this morning."

"But Pa, Johnny only comes but once a year! And we been thinkin'bout that river—seems like forever."

Ma spoke up. "Wonder if it bears any resemblance to the river Jordan in the Good Book? Wouldn't mind setting eyes on it myself. 'Course, I never could leave the cooking and the baby. . . ."

"I'd say it was a sight prettier than the River Jordan, Mrs. McDonald," joined in old Mr. Stuart. "Bible's set in desert country, after all. Israelites referred to it as the land of milk and honey, but that was only because they'd never seen any better. If the Lord were set on coming back to walk among his people today, he'd surely find no lovelier river to preach along than the Ohio. A fair inspiration it is, to the godly, seeing such beauty."

Pa had finally simmered down some. He carefully polished off his plate before making his decision, though. "Heard nothing but 'the river' these past three years since Johnny put the idea into Maggie's head. Guess I'll never hear the end of it if I don't let the youngsters have a look. You can take my compass, Johnny, and Ma can pack some dinner for you. See you're back before sunset, though. Got no mind to go chasing after you through the forest in the dark."

Then Charlie wanted to come too, but was finally persuaded he'd have a better time getting stories from old Mr. Stuart.

"Can we have the concertina, too, sir?"

"What concertina?" thundered Pa.

Johnny and I and the boys disappeared fast to tend to the animals before we could be pulled into that fray. We finished with the chores in record time, but waited till we saw Pa storming off to the fields before we emerged from the chicken house and went to get the food from Ma. Then we were off into the forest— Johnny, with the compass and an ax, leading the way; the boys, following him with water bags; and me, bringing up the rear with the knapsack full of food.

Seemed like we slogged through those trees for hours, getting hotter and damper all the time. Woods just kept getting darker and thicker. We made enough noise to raise the dead, so of course we didn't see much in the way of wildlife, just a snake or two curled up here and there on rocks, and lots of mosquitoes. Wished I'd had some of that crane's bill along to crush up and chase them off. We did spot signs of animal life, though. There were deer tracks, like the kind we found near our fields some mornings, and once Johnny even pointed out tracks he thought belonged to wolves.

Johnny just kept glancing at the compass and making a trail due south, every so often stopping to gash a marker in a stump or tree trunk so's we'd have it easier getting home. I had no idea what the time might be and felt I'd been walking forever, least my legs were telling me that, when suddenly a little more light started to creep between the trees. We all kind of rushed up on top of Johnny and broke through the woods and just stared.

We were on top of a rise and down below us was the river. The boys and I just flopped down on our bellies, huffing and puffing and looking. Johnny smiled a little smile, and his eyes took on that faraway look as he followed the bends of the water out of sight to the west.

I finally picked myself up, pulled off the knapsack and started in dividing up the bread and cheese and beef jerky. I looked up at the sky.

"It's already past noon and we've been walking since about seven. Guess we'd better eat before we start back."

Abe looked up from the river. "Not goin' nowhere 'til I see a boat or raft come floatin' down that river like Johnny promised."

"Me neither," piped in Aaron.

Johnny sat down next to me and reached for his portion. "Guess we've got about an hour to rest before we'll have to be getting back. The getting here took a little longer than I estimated, and it'll be harder on the way home. We'll be tired and not plowing through those trees as fast."

I ate contentedly, with my eyes always on the blue ribbon of water below us. "It is lovely," I said finally. "Wish Ma could see it."

"Been waiting for your word of approval, Meg," said Johnny. "Doesn't it just take you right along with it—to beyond? Same as our star last night." And he touched my hand.

Just then the boys let out a whoop. "Boat comin' 'round the bend!"

Right then and there I gave up on trying to be calm and grown up. Dropped my food where I was sitting and rushed over to join the boys. Sure enough! It was a boat—or more like a raft. Kind of squarish, with sails pulling it closer and closer to our view. Abe and Aaron started in jumping and waving and shouting and pretty soon I was doing the same, till the tiny people out there in the middle of the river started waving back. I was plumb hoarse by the time we'd followed that raft out of sight down the river. Went back to Johnny, brushed the ants off my bread, and continued to eat. He laughed then.

"You are something, Meg girl. Half woman, half child. Hope you never lose the child part altogether."

Had an inkling of what he was talking about then, but the blush running over my face pushed all thinking out of my head. I reached for a water bag and busied myself with a drink to hide my confusion. Then the boys were clamoring finally for their food.

Didn't see anything else moving on that river, 'cept a big old bird swooping kind of low over it, probably looking for a fish. It was enough. We were all satisfied. When Johnny said it was time to be starting back, no one complained. The boys just headed off into the woods. I took my time and turned back for one more long look. Johnny had waited with me, a hand touching mine lightly.

"Just trying to drink it all in once more. To remember," I said.

"Someday you'll see it again. And more. Just with me," he whispered. Then he spun around and headed back into the deep woods.

It was near sunset when we came at last to our clearing. Pa was fussing with the horses in the pasture when we broke through, and I saw a look of relief cross his face.

"Praise the Lord. You're all back—and in one piece."

I went up to him then and touched his arm. "Thank you, Pa. It was a rare event and I do thank you for allowing us the opportunity."

I could see his eyes smiling, but he just said, "Get into the house with you. Your mother's been a wreck with the worrying all day."

"Yes, Pa." And I was even more pleased going back to the house, 'cause I knew that Pa had done a piece of worrying as well.

After a few bites of supper the boys got their energy back and set in to giving Ma and the rest of us a blow-by-blow account of the wonders of the river. I just sat and listened, with a small smile of remembrance on my face. And when the boys brought out Pa's Bible after the meal, he set in to reading about John the Baptist and his work on the shores of the River Jordan. The boys were almost asleep before he finished. And Johnny and I sat out on the porch without a lantern or book that night. I figured we had enough good pictures in our heads already.

When they left the next day I had Johnny's Shakespeare in my hands and Pa had bought a little book of stories about George Washington's life especially for Charlie. Charlie was proud as a peacock at having his very own first book, and I guessed I'd have to start him in on his lessons now, too. No sense in waiting any longer when he was so all-fired willing. Just look at all the time I'd wasted till I was ten.

I gave old Mr. Stuart a hug and Ma sent him off with some soft biscuits and a pudding. Johnny just looked at me from a distance, almost scared, he seemed, to come any closer. Felt just about the same myself. Next year never seemed so far away.

Then I sat down on the porch steps, with Dog kind of keening a little at my feet till I couldn't hear the wagon any more.

CHAPTER 7

IT WAS LATE AUGUST next, and I was out in the fields helping Pa and the boys to harvest the last of the corn when Johnny came walking up to us, head and shoulders above the corn.

"Johnny!" I dropped everything and ran up to him. "Got your Pa settled in on the porch?"

He didn't answer. Just looked at me.

"Johnny! Whatever is the matter?"

"Buried Pa two weeks back over in Athens. Next to the college. Thought he'd be happy there." He looked like he was going to cry. I *was* crying.

"Oh, Johnny!" I walked right into his arms and he stood there holding me, the two of us wet with each other's tears.

"What in tarnation's going on here?" It was my pa, of course.

Johnny and I backed away from each other, then he saw our faces.

"The old man's gone, then." It was a statement of fact.

"Yes, sir," Johnny finally spoke. "And Mabel, too.

When Pa went, she just sort of folded up her legs and gave up. Buried her near to Pa. Thought the Lord wouldn't mind, and maybe they'd be giving each other some company.''

Pa pulled off his hat and wiped his face some. Never saw him so near to a real emotion before. Then he put his hat back on. "World's the lesser for his moving on, but I reckon the Lord and his angels gonna have some rare entertainment." He looked around at the corn. "Better finish bringing this in afore supper. Time and the devil wait for no man."

Johnny and I walked back to sit on the porch. I could hear Ma kind of sniffling and blowing her nose inside, and little Sarah racing around laughing, not knowing what had happened.

I reached for Johnny's hand and we just sat together very quietly, Felicity curled up at our feet, until Johnny was able to talk about it.

"Just woke up one morning, Meg, and started in to fix our breakfast. When I went to shake my Pa awake, he wasn't there anymore. Just his cold old body. Felicity jumped up to lick him, like she did, but it didn't help. Poor dog began to howl like her heart was breaking, and I howled right along."

I squeezed his hand a little. "It was a mercy he went like that, just in his sleep."

"Oh, I know his body was finished, Meg, but there was so much left in that head of his! So much he could have taught me yet."

"He knew you were just about finished growing, Johnny. I think he hung on hard till he knew you could manage things on your own."

"And he was talking about visiting here, Meg. He enjoyed you all a powerful lot. Enjoyed setting his mind against your father's and watching you and the boys grow into learning. He was powerful pleased with you, Meg. Even bought a book specially for you this winter. An English ladies' book, by an English lady, Jane Austen. Said he figured you'd be mature enough to enjoy its nuances. Even said the heroine of the piece reminded him of you in a way, and I know he meant it as a compliment—to your high spirits."

The tears were streaming down my face again, but I tried to ignore them and asked what book his Pa had had in mind.

"*Pride and Prejudice*. I'll bring it up for you after supper. Pa would've wanted us to continue our readings together. In fact, Pa kind of took it for granted that we'd be doing a whole lot of things together for the rest of our lives. Told me himself I'd find no better mate for life than you, Meg. But I already knew that."

I held his hand tighter.

"Meg." He freed his hand and moved both of his to hold my face before his own. "Meg, I mean to ask your father for your hand. I know you're not more than sixteen, but I've waited so long for you. Are you willing?"

"Oh, yes, Johnny! I've been willing since that first day you came around our bend seven years ago."

We looked in each other's eyes for the longest time and my tears dried up. I figured I was woman enough to take on Johnny now. Pa felt differently.

At supper that night Ma set an extra place for old Mr. Stuart, and we all sat staring at it, wishing he was there to liven up the proceedings. Pa read from the Bible about the Lord's resurrection, and made a few remarks about how, sooner or later, he figured we'd all meet up again in heaven with Johnny's pa. Ma and I just kept dabbing at our eyes, but Johnny took it right manly. Abe and Aaron were silent and only Charlie kept asking questions.

"But *why* won't he ever be back? I *liked* him!"

"Hush, Charlie," said Ma. "He's dead and gone. Angels took him up to heaven to keep them company."

"Like my pet hog 'Towser'?"

"Sort of like that, Charlie."

"Oh." And I could see him set in to thinking about that.

Pa put the Bible away and got ready to shut up the animals for the night.

"Sir?"

He stopped at the door. "Yes, Johnny?"

"I know this may not be the best moment, but I've got to get it out."

"Whatever it is, get it off your chest, son."

"About Meg, sir. Seems like she's finally just about grown up."

I saw my ma and the boys sort of stop in the middle of things and perk up their ears.

"Yes, Johnny?"

"I dearly want to marry her, sir. I'd cherish her, I would, and see that she kept your ways and the Lord's, too. Traveling around like Pa and I did, we never went to church much. But we studied the Bible; we knew—I know—Jesus and His way. Please, may I have your permission?"

Pa just stood there a moment. "The girl's not more than sixteen-and-a-half, Johnny. She looks grown, but I think another year of waiting would do more good than harm. For yourself as well. Think about it, Johnny. You need some time to find your own ways without your pa, spread your wings a little and learn to fly on your own. Wouldn't be a favor to you to take you from one obligation and put you right into another afore you're ready." This said, he made ready to leave again.

"Pa!" I cried out. He looked at me.

"I know your heart's willing, Maggie. Known that for some time. But my word stands."

"Yes, Pa." Then I had a thought. "Maybe Johnny could winter with us Pa, 'stead of by himself in the lonesome city. He'd be a proper help about the place. We could lodge him in the loft."

"No, Maggie. He's a man now. Got to have his proper period of mourning and growing into *knowing* he's a man on his own." And Pa walked out the door.

The room came to life again, but I just stood there, hurting.

"Get out on to the porch with Johnny, Maggie. I'll do the tidying up tonight."

"Thank you, Ma."

We sat gently rocking on the swing, watching the twilight darken into night. Johnny finally spoke.

"Guess I'll do my wintering in Cincinnati this year. Won't seem so far from you somehow. Come spring I'll set out a bit into new territory, maybe Indiana, Kentucky. I'll come for you in the autumn."

I felt bereft. "You won't forget me, Johnny?"

"How could I, Meg girl? You know full well you're my heart's desire. Feel just like Romeo tonight. I've got my Juliet well within sights, yet can't lay a hand on her."

"You think my Pa's right, Johnny?"

He ran strong, fine fingers through his glorious curls. Then he sighed. "Your father's strong on good sense, Meg. My heart says he's wrong, but my mind knows he's talking the truth. Guess I've got to know that I can make it on my own before tying you down. Till two weeks ago I never knew how much I depended on my father. It's been desolate traveling without him. My new horse is a sight younger than Mabel, though, and good and strong. Guess that's some consolation. And I've got the dog here," he reached down to pat Felicity. "Least she's something to talk to."

"What can I do, Johnny, while I'm waiting?"

"Well," he grinned finally. "You can make me a new wedding shirt. Guess I haven't paid much attention to my bodily dress these past few years." He glanced at his worn shirt and trousers a bit ruefully. "But I sure would like to look nice on my wedding day."

"Oh, Johnny! I'll make you the most *beautiful* shirt!" And finally having something to put my energy into, I rushed into the house to get my sewing things. I came out armed to the teeth, and with a lantern to see by. "Stand up, Johnny!"

"Hey! I didn't mean tonight!"

"I'm just going to measure you up for some cloth from Locust Grove. Now stand still, and don't jiggle so."

"Yes, ma'am!" but he was finally smiling. And when I got done with the measuring, he took the lantern and led me down to his wagon.

"Something else you can do for me, Meg." He carefully revealed the rows of books and started in browsing amongst them, pulling out a volume here and there.

"Whatever are you doing, Johnny Stuart?"

"If I'm going to take on a new partner in my bookselling enterprises, I'll want her to be well read. It'll be your job to sweet-talk the wives and children, while I work on the men of the family."

"But, Johnny, isn't that a funny kind of attitude to be taking to your customers?"

"Don't mean any disrespect toward them Meg, but they take a little convincing at times to know a good thing when it's set before them. Just part of the business. And the Lord said to let your light shine, Meg. Just want to trim up your wick a little. There's certainly no harm in bringing our light into new homes. Changed both our lives after our first visit to you." He set down his handful of books a moment and took me by the shoulders. "Understand, Meg. I never hope to be a rich man. At least not in the coin of the realm. Pa and I, we never made more than enough to keep us going from year to year, and I don't expect that to change any. If you finally take me on next year, it'll be for the riches of my mind, the riches that together we can give to each other."

"It will also be because I love you, Johnny. For you and your mind. Nice to take the book's binding into account on occasion, too."

"Meg, love. You are a wonder." And then he was kissing me good and proper, not like the little touches last summer. His lips were as strong as the rest of his body, and seemed to fit mine just right. It was a glorious preface to things to come, and I sure didn't want to let go. Finally he eased up with a sigh, untangled our arms, and went back to choosing books. He soon had a sizeable pile sorted out and we returned to the porch to look through them.

Johnny chose the first. "Now this one is Oliver Goldsmith's *The Vicar of Wakefield*. Kind of a novel of manners and reform. Shows you a little of the life in England about eighty years back, too. And here's your *Pride and Prejudice*. You're surely going to love that." He picked another from the pile. "This is Scott's first novel proper. He got into writing it when his verse stories sort of slacked off and he needed the money. It's *Waverly*, the story of the Stuart uprising in 1745 that brought your great-grandparents to the new world. . . . I'm also thinking a little philosophy won't be amiss, so I'm leaving with you Rousseau's *Emile*, translated from the French. Along similar lines, I'm throwing in Pope's *Essay on Man*. Believe it or not, he's the one who first got me interested in seeing some Indians. I'll never forget my pa's reading from it to me." And he closed his eyes and recited from memory:

Lo! the poor Indian, whose untutored mind
Sees God in clouds, or hears him in the wind;
His soul proud Science never taught to stray
Far as the solar walk, or milky way;

Yet simple Nature to his hope has given,
Behind the cloud-topped hill, an humbler heaven.

"How lovely!"

"So I thought then, and still do. Pope and Gold-smith are perennial good sellers for us, so you should have a working knowledge of them. Let's see; what else have we here?" He selected another volume. "This is *Don Quixote*, from the Spanish. It's already been responsible for some poorer American copies, like Brackenridge's *Modern Chivalry*, but I won't trouble you with that. Best to stick with the original." He went on into some tomes of science and astronomy, but by that time my head was already reeling.

"Enough, Johnny! I spent all last year on Shakespeare. However will I get through all these and still do my work?"

"Not to worry, Meg. All these together aren't worth one of Shakespeare's plays. Your year was well spent." He pushed aside the pile. "Just want you to see the possibilities, Meg."

I snuggled next to him. "I *do* see them, Johnny."

He tugged playfully at the long braid of hair falling down my back, then touched the fronds that had slipped loose around my face.

"So do I, Meg. So do I. Can't wait till I have the right to unbraid this hair and see it all spread out in glory." He kissed my neck. "And I shouldn't be even thinking it, no less saying it, but that goes for the rest of you, too."

I felt the heat rising from somewhere in the middle of me and going right up to my face. "Hush, Johnny. What if Pa heard?"

"Your pa knows my intentions are honorable. The Good Lord made marriage for that very reason. Nothing indecent about a man's loving his wife, or wishing for his wife-to-be, for that matter." He fumbled around his neck for a moment, then pulled off a golden chain with a little golden cross suspended from it. I held my breath while he slowly lowered it over my head and around my neck.

"This is the only thing my mother left for me before she disappeared, Meg. I want you to have it. As a betrothal gift."

"Oh, Johnny!" There were tears in my eyes again. But this time they were tears of joy.

"I'll wear it always, Johnny, next to my heart."

He caught my hands and kissed my fingers, one by one. "Next time I see you I'll be bringing a little golden ring to match, for your finger." Then he stood up and pulled me up with him. "And now you'll be going to sleep while I can still keep my good counsel."

He led me to the door and bade me goodnight with a gentle kiss.

Didn't do much sleeping that night with all the thinking, and I don't believe Johnny did, either. He looked plumb tuckered out over breakfast the next morning. And then he was harnessing up his new horse, making ready to leave. We all stood there watching, kind of silent. Finally Pa spoke up.

"Don't tell me, Johnny, that you're not going to try and sell me a book before you leave. You'll have your father turning in his grave next."

Well, that kind of livened things up. Johnny opened up the books with a grin and the old flourish and gave Pa a good spiel on his latest agricultural treatise, and didn't Pa just buy it! Ma and I had already filled up the wagon with more preserves and such than Johnny could eat by himself in a year, so I guess he was about as ready as he ever would be to take on the world.

I made myself smile as I walked with him down to the bend, but inside I was crying so it hurt. He took my hand a moment before climbing up the wagon.

"God bless you and keep you for me, Meg."

"And you, too, Johnny."

Then he was gone on his adventuring, and me left to live through the year. Almost wished I'd been a boy then, till I remembered with a grin that *that* surely would've put a crimp in our plans some.

I have to say that that autumn and winter were the longest of my life. We went to camp meeting as usual in October and there was Hildy, no longer living at home, but proud as punch showing off her new husband Bernd at the meeting. He seemed nice enough, in a big, blond, farmerish sort of way. Put me in mind of a huge ox Pa used to have.

'Course Hildy had filled out some, too. Must be all those dumplings her Ma taught her to make. Not to mention the mashed potatoes and shoo-fly pie. She looked different in other ways, too, more knowing-like. I must say that viper jealousy gave me a good nip then. But I remembered myself and congratulated the two of them, showing off my betrothal present and mentioning things to come. Hildy surely was a good sort. She gave me a hug at my news and said as how it was well worth the waiting, for there surely wasn't anything like married bliss. She didn't blush none at that, but her new husband did a bit.

After the religion and the gossip and the buying at Locust Grove, we went back home and set into making my "trousseau." Lovely word, that. Got it from Jane Austen. Sounded much more definite than "hope chest."

I wasn't forgetting Johnny's request, either. Ma helped me to pick some fine white linen at the store, and after I sewed it together, I spent many a night stitching embroidery all over it. Ma wasn't sure it was quite the thing, but I had decided that a "story" shirt was appropriate for Johnny. So as not to be too garish, I made my pictures all in white. There was the wagon, and Mabel pulling it, and Felicity running alongside. Then there was old Mr. Stuart doffing his hat with a fine bow, and Johnny beside him, doing the same. On one sleeve I added a little girl watching, with the only touch of color. I gave her red braids. On the other sleeve I stitched a little log cabin, like ours had looked so long ago. Pa just gave me a look every time he saw me working on that shirt, but he didn't say anything.

When I wasn't sewing or cooking or looking after the youngsters or giving lessons or tending to my other chores, I'd take up one of Johnny's books. Mostly I read them by lamplight in my room at night, long after everyone else was asleep. Can't say that I understood them all at first reading, but I kept at it, and bits and pieces started coming together in my head.

Then it got on close to Christmas, and I put the books aside to spend all my free time making the place festive. Made some real pretty corn-husk dolls for Sarah, and snuck out to the barn with Pa on occasion to help paint up some wooden toys he'd been cobbling for the boys. Even did a big piece of embroidery for Ma to hang on the wall, and Pa helped me frame it. It was a colorful picture of our house in summer, everything gay and blossoming. And around it I'd stitched the words, "God Bless Our Home." Put in everybody in a row out in front of the house, too, from Pa on down to little Sarah. Came out kind of nice.

Then it was the eve of Christmas, and Pa and the boys brought in a great green tree and we decorated it with cookies and popped corn. Sure wished Johnny had been there to see it. Before we went to sleep that night, Pa let the boys do the Bible reading. 'Course they chose the Nativity. Took it in turns, they did, reading from all the Gospels. Even Charlie picked out a few words.

In the morning we shared gifts, and Ma roasted up a fat goose for our dinner. I was a little sad, then, thinking this might be my last Christmas shared with the family. But I didn't say anything that could put a damper on the pleasant spirits that abounded.

Spring came and I started in getting real anxious. What if Johnny headed west without me? What if some girl in Cincinnati had caught his eye over the wintering months? He'd said he'd be pretty busy between the library and the museum and the lecturing they had there—not to mention keeping out of the way of all those streets filled with hogs—but still the worry was there.

Right into the summer, I tended my garden and my chores with half an eye always on the road coming up 'round the bend. I have to say that Ma and Pa were patience personified. Once in a while I could see them eying me, then kind of giving each other a look, but they didn't say a thing, bless them. I was real glad then that Ma had little Sarah to start in raising up to help her. Another year or two, and she'd begin to be right useful about the place.

Well, it got on to August and I could truthfully say there was a general strain in the family. Even Charlie took to asking when Johnny would finally get here. And still he didn't come. I couldn't face another book or another piece of needlework.

By the last day of the month of August, I was just spending my spare time sitting on the porch gazing down the road. Then it started in to rain. Rained for days, hard and cold. Pa was frantic for his crop and didn't pay me any further mind.

On the fouth of September, it was still coming down like Noah's flood when I looked out the door and saw Johnny's wagon. *Thank You, Father!* I flew out that door into that rain so fast that Ma dropped the pie she was pulling from the oven.

"Johnny! Johnny! Johnny!" I was in his arms, dripping wet.

"Meg, love!"

Ma finally pulled us into the house and out of the rain.

We stood there, sopping and grinning. Suddenly, as if remembering, Johnny doffed his hat and gave Ma and me a bow.

"Forgive my manners, ladies. I was quite taken by the moment. Would've been here days sooner, but it took me a week to track down a minister." He stopped, then pointed out the door. "Here he comes now."

We rushed to the door in time to see a lank, very wet man pull himself off his horse, grab his saddlebags, and head for the house. In a moment he was inside, shaking himself.

He offered his hand to Ma. "Jacob Young, ma'am, rider for the Lord."

Ma beamed. "And welcome you are, all of you. Maggie, go ring the bell for your Pa and the boys. This would be an Event."

That night the preacher offered grace at our table, then dug in like he'd never seen food before. Johnny had entrusted Pa with my golden ring, and the ceremony was set for the next morning. We all sat up together some after the meal while the Reverend Young gave a little homily about entering the married state and the Lord's entrusting to the newlyweds the job of raising new souls in His image. Johnny sat very still next to me. I longed to reach for his hand, but somehow I thought it wouldn't appear seemly.

After he'd done his duty by Johnny and me, Pa asked the preacher how he'd come to his calling.

"Well, I'll tell you, sir. Had my doubts, I did, till one night the Savior himself appeared to me with the Book of Life in His hands and showed me my name inscribed there. Gave me such a start, it did, that I was unconscious for hours. And when I finally awoke and realized I'd been truly translated from the power of darkness into the Kingdom of God's dear Son, I fainted dead away again.''

Pa looked properly impressed. ''Mighty similar to Paul,'' he mused. Then, ''Never saw you round these parts before.''

''No, sir. Just passing through, I was, on my way down to the big revival in Kentucky. Happy to be of service here to you and the Lord on my way.''

''Hear tell they've had some powerful fine meetings down that way,'' commented Pa.

''Indeed. Though not quite like the old days forty years back when we'd get more than twenty thousand souls to preach to.'' He sighed audibly. ''Sometimes I fear religion's getting a little *too* civilized, like these parts of the country. Still, I intend to work up a little thunder and lightning for the Lord, I do.''

At his pause, Ma was sending me off to bed early so that I'd be well rested for the morning. Hated to let Johnny out of my sight for another instant, but there wasn't any choice. I walked up the stairs with half an ear on Pa's and the preacher's conversation.

When I woke the next morning the rains had stopped, and the sun was streaming down in all its glory. I eased out of my bed real slow and stretched with a smile. This was the day the Lord had made! He was surely smiling down on Johnny and me.

I went to my hope chest and carefully removed my wedding dress, smoothing out the wrinkles. It was a lovely pale blue, with darker blue satin trimmings that Ma and I had pieced on. I carefully laid it on the bed, then went downstairs to get some water. It was early yet, and I had time to wash my hair and bathe before the ceremony. I peeked out the window near my jelly cupboard. Johnny was out there by the well, doing the same thing. I watched him for a minute, remembering the other times I'd done the same. Then Ma bustled out of her bedroom with Sarah.

"Good morning, daughter," she beamed. Then she handed me a little bar of something. "Got it for you in Locust Grove last autumn. Genuine lilac-scented soap. Been saving it for The Day."

"Thank you, Ma!" Then I gave her a good long hug and we both kind of sniffled a little.

"Just wanted you to know, Maggie. Life with your father's been hard, but good. I got myself a good, strong, God-fearing man, and wish you the same with Johnny. Your life's bound to be a little different, with all the wandering, and I guess sooner or later you'll be going further west and leaving us behind. Just try and be for him the kind of woman I brought you up to be. Be true to your upbringing, and to the Lord."

"Yes, Ma." We looked at each other for a long while, then she gave me a little shove.

"Get upstairs now with the washtub and make yourself pretty. Every woman's got that right on her wedding day."

Well, I gave her a little smile and did just that. Pretty soon Ma came upstairs and helped me into my dress. Then we walked downstairs. Johnny and Pa and the boys were decked out in their best duds. Johnny was looking a little nervous, but very elegant in my shirt. It suited him, somehow, just like I'd known it would. When he saw me coming, he pulled a frock coat over it, so that all I could see of the embroidery was him and his Pa, doffing their hats, like the first time we'd set eyes on them.

Everyone shuffled around a bit till finally the preacher started in to organize the proceedings. He gave a little speech in front of the fireplace about my promising to honor and obey Johnny, and to Johnny he talked about forsaking all others for me. Johnny's eyes were on mine the whole time, and I had some trouble digesting all the words. Then Johnny took my

110

hand and we started in with the vows. Truly beautiful, they were. And I was so wrapped up in them that I hardly heard myself saying "I do." But I guess I did, because there was Johnny's golden ring on my finger, and Johnny gave me a sweet kiss in front of everyone.

Before you know it, everyone was hugging us, and then Ma set in to put a feast upon the table. Pa slipped out just then to check his fields and returned to remark, casual-like, that it looked as though the Lord had spared his grain and there'd be a good harvest after all. Then Pa really loosened up, gave a big smile, and toasted Johnny and me with fresh cider.

It was near three by the mantel clock when Pa and Johnny had all my things stowed in the wagon. The whole family was lined up and one by one I hugged and kissed them all, tears in my eyes. Finally, Johnny hauled me away, hoisted me up on the wagon, took his seat beside me, and together we rode that wagon down the rise and around the bend to a new life.

Part II

THE ROAD

CHAPTER 8

HILDY WAS SURE RIGHT about marriage. Seemed to do both Johnny and me a world of good. Of course, there were the getting-used-to things of living on the road, like learning how to set up a good campfire on pleasant nights, and bathing and doing laundry in available streams. Didn't take long to readjust my sights to the road beyond instead of the boundaries of Pa's hundred-odd acres. I must say I delighted in the change of scenery, much to Johnny's pleasure. We just went rolling along for about a week till Johnny deemed it time to do a little business.

Late one afternoon we spied a pleasant little farm ahead of us. Johnny gave me a look.

"Ready, Meg?"

"Ready as I'll ever be."

He smiled. "Here goes, then."

We drove up to that farm and planted the wagon nice as you please between the house and the barn. Curious chickens and a few youngsters scrambled about, eying us. The husband and wife of the place emerged and Johnny helped me down.

Holding my hand, he doffed his hat, made a nice little bow to which I added a curtsy he'd taught me, and started in.

"Pleasant afternoon to you, sir and madam. Allow me to make introductions. John Stuart and wife, purveyors of books inspirational and educational, moralistic and fanciful, at your service."

Well, they kind of gawked, and I kind of grinned. I must say that it was from that point on that I really felt like Johnny's wife. In another few minutes we had slabs of fresh apple pie and glasses of cool well water to drink. We tucked that down, then got into passing on the bits of gossip Johnny had picked up on his recent travels. That went over real well, sort of warmed things up and put a mark of bona fide on us, so to speak. Well, in less time that it takes to tell it, Johnny was showing off the books and selling three volumes of them. Pleased I am to say that I was responsible for convincing the lady of the house, Mrs. Dowell, to purchase *Mother Goose's Melody: or Sonnets for the Cradle*, printed from the English version by Isaiah Thomas of Worcester, Massachusetts, some years back. I pointed out with a certain pride of knowledge that not only did it have verses in it for her children, it also contained some sweet songs by William Shakespeare suitable for the delectation of the entire family. Of course I had to give the children a proper sampling, explaining all the while who Mother Goose was. They did take to "Hey Diddle Diddle, the Cat and the Fiddle" right off and were soon dancing around singing it.

We didn't get invited to dinner, but we pulled away an hour or two later with fresh eggs, fresh bread, and coins jingling merrily in Johnny's pocket. We traveled another hour or two until sunset, when Dickens, the horse, spotted a nice piece of grass and decided it was time for supper. It was a beautiful autumn evening, and I fried up some of Pa's bacon with the eggs and we had a cozy meal. Afterward, I sat snuggled next to Johnny against the wagon wheel and he picked out the stars in the sky for me. I sighed in total contentment.

"Meg?"

"Yes, Johnny?"

"You did a good job back at that farm."

"Thank you, Johnny." Bliss.

"Meg?"

"Yes, Johnny?"

"How would you like to winter further west this year?"

"How far west?" I asked, suddenly suspicious.

"Oh, just another three hundred miles or so. Chicago, Illinois."

"Chicago?"

"Hear they've got a nice-sized town there now. Maybe fifteen thousand people. And it's set on Lake Michigan. Biggest lake you'll ever see. More like an ocean, it is, from things I've heard."

"Can we buy books there, Johnny?"

"Must be books in a town that size. But just in case, we can stop over in Cincinnati on the way and fill up the holes a little."

"Where will that put us for the spring, Johnny?"

I could feel him grin in the dark. "In a direct line south and west to the Mississippi River."

"And Independence, Missouri, I suppose."

He gave me a little hug. "You married me knowing I was a wanderer, Meg."

I sighed. "Sure did. And no regrets. Just didn't expect the 'further west' would come this soon."

"Meg, the tales I've heard about the Oregon country you just would not believe. Trees so tall you can't see their tops. Mountain lakes gleaming with snow and teeming with fish. And peaceful Indians."

"Not for long, with all the Easterners heading out to take over their lands."

"Don't see how we'd get in the way much. The way

116

I understand it, most of the Indians live on the shores of the Pacific Ocean, and support themselves by fishing. That leaves a lot of free country inland.''

"But, Johnny, you don't mean you never anticipate settling down with a piece of our own ground, do you?''

"Not exactly, but there's bound to be families hungering for books.''

"But that country's just being explored, way I understand it. It'll be ten, twenty years before it'll be able to support us from bookselling. How will we live in the meantime?''

"Don't know for sure yet, but something's bound to come to me.''

"And how will you get books out there? It's not like you can just travel over to Philadelphia or Cincinnati when the need arises. Almost have to print them ourselves.''

"Well, hear they have got a powerful lot of trees out there. You might just have the right idea, Meg.'' He had that dreamy sound in his voice again. "We could buy us a little printing press, and some type. . . .''

"Last I heard, things like that cost money, Johnny.''

He paid me no heed. "Might even do us some translations of the Bible for the Indians. . . .''

"Got to know their language first. And I never have heard of an Indian alphabet. What if they haven't got a written language?''

"We could help them devise one.''

"If they got by, happy, with just fishing and living all this time, how do you know they want one?''

"Once *you* picked up the word-hunger, couldn't keep you in enough books.''

"That's different.''

"Is it? What makes you so different from an Indian squaw, cooking and sewing and keeping her family?''

117

"Honestly, Johnny. You do ask the most vexing questions!"

"You think about that. But not too hard this very minute, not on this fine night." And he began to gently unbraid my waist-length hair.

We hit paydirt for sure at the farm where we stopped the following day. We pulled up in front of the house like before. Just a little log cabin it was, with not many improvements as yet. Turned out only a farmer lived there, unwed. A little strange, he was, maybe just from the loneliness. His name was Joe Scraggs and he looked to be a little younger than Pa. He was dirty for sure, with matted shoulder-length hair and a beard that hung down to his chest. And I could see he had the vermin problem, 'cause he just stood there a-scratching and a-scratching, the whole time Johnny gave his spiel. Finally I could stand it no longer and went into the wagon to fetch some of my dried herbs Ma had sent me off with. I came out of our wagon and set right to work.

"Mr. Scraggs," says I, "it's not my job, but I can see you sure do need a woman's touch around here. If you've got a washtub to haul out, do so, please, and let me just cook up some of my herbs on your fire. If you've a mind to rid yourself of your itch, I can do it."

Well, Scraggs and Johnny both gave me some peculiar looks, but there wasn't anything to be done but what I asked, so before you know it, he was stripping and scrubbing himself down with my concoction. He came out looking visibly better, but I could see that the hair and beard were still teeming. Wasn't anything for it but to get Johnny's razor and shave him down to the scalp and chin skin, then rub ointments all over. By this time I knew we had a full day's project going for us, so I upended his tub, filled it clean again and started in on scrubbing his clothes and linens. Made Johnny throw his pallet into the fire and sent them both out for fresh hay for a clean one. Then his cabin needed a good going over. Never did see a man needed a woman more than that one.

Well, come suppertime there we still were, all three of us working with spirit. I'd thought to put some potatoes into his coals, and fried up some nice slabs of ham. He had lots of ham, hanging all over from the rafters, it was. He also had an odd collection of instruments decorating his wall. When we finally sat down to a prayer and supper, I finally got to ask him about them.

He nodded at the array. "They be my one joy in life, Missus. Seems like anything I pick up makes music for me. Many's the night I've entertained myself and the bugs," here he smiled a bit ruefully. "Guess I can manage without the last. You are a whirlwind for sure. Place hasn't been so clean since my wife died in childbirth these long four years since."

"Why don't you get yourself another?" I asked practically. "Four years is a long time to be without."

"Where? Haven't been off the place since."

"I looked at Johnny. "Seems to me you said Cincinnati's not that far from here."

"Couple of days' trip."

"How'm I going to leave my livestock? Can't fend for themselves that long. Cow'd dry up and pigs' run wild."

"Mr. Scraggs, there must be hundreds of women looking for a good, *clean* man who can raise pigs fine as you can. This ham is delicious, probably better than my Pa's, even."

He beamed some under his now shiny dome. When his hair started in coming back he'd probably be a fine figure of a man.

"It's all in the curing, Missus. 'Course you got to

119

start off with a good animal to begin with. I smokes my hams on a corncob fire."

"My Pa always used hickory wood, but I'll sure pass your experience on to him next we meet. Pa might argue the point, but he never questions success."

He finished up his plate, wiping up the last juices with the johnnycake I'd fried up at the hearth. "How about some thinking music?" he asked.

Thought he'd never get that far. I watched with bated breath while he took a fiddle down from the wall, then lit into it. Simply amazing music came out.

"Johnny," I whispered, "have you still got your Pa's concertina?"

He nodded yes, looking bemused again.

"Can you play it?"

"Of course. Just never came up at your place."

"Fetch it, please."

Mr. Scraggs got so excited when he saw Johnny's concertina that he took down another instrument from the wall and handed it to me.

"Whatever am I to do with this?" I looked at the strange thing before me, sort of like a long-handled drum with strings attached.

"Play it! Not hard at all." And he briefly demonstrated.

"It's a banjo! Heard it at a minstrel show in Cincinnati before my wife passed on. Poor woman couldn't drag me out of the place till I'd bartered for one of my own."

Well, my sound wasn't like his, but I gave it my best, and before we knew it, we had some mighty interesting music resounding from that cabin. That banjo tickled me mightily. Every so often Mr. Scraggs would put down one instrument and experiment with another. His mandolin—Johnny pointed out that it was akin to one of Shakespeare's lutes—was ever so sweet, and the autoharp was poignant. We must've gone on for hours, till finally we all sort of stopped at once.

"Trade you everything I've got for that wife of yours, Johnny Stuart."

Johnny looked startled for a moment; then, taking it as the compliment it was meant to be, started to grin. "Like to oblige you, Mr. Scraggs, but I'm just now getting her broke in to my way of liking."

"Thought as much. Got another deal for you then." And he stopped to scratch at his head automatically, till he realized there wasn't anything left to scratch at. "You folks stay on here for a week till I go and fetch me a new wife. Look after the place, like. Buy every book in your wagon when I get back, and throw in the banjo for the missus, too. Been having a yen for a few good books."

Johnny just stared for a moment.

"Look here, I can afford it." He went over to a chest and pulled out a bag of gold coins. He jiggled them provocatively. "Just name your price. I guess you two maybe saved my life today. Thought for sure the Lord had forsaken me for good afore you pulled up. Almost ready to pack it all in, I was, pigs and all."

Still speechless, Johnny was trying, uselessly, to clear his throat.

"Seems to me we can make some kind of an arrangement, Mr. Scraggs," I piped up. "Lord never meant for a man to be despairing like that. You head off for the city first thing tomorrow morning. And see that you pick yourself a good worker, a godly woman. This place will blossom for you."

Right about then Johnny pulled me out to our wagon, his head shaking like it would come off.

"What am I going to do with you, Meg girl? Are you going to try and save every poor lout we meet up with?"

"Anybody can play music like that is not a lout, Johnny."

"Well, maybe you've got something there." Still shaking his head, he prepared for bed.

Scraggs was gone before we pulled ourselves out of our bunks the next morning, and there we were with a farm to tend to.

"I still don't understand you, Meg," Johnny almost complained. "You haven't been off of your farm for more than ten days and here you go and tie us all down on another. That man may never come back." He looked around him some. "If *I* had this place, *I'd* never come back for sure."

I followed his gaze around the poor spread. "You've got something there, Johnny, but I figure it's just poor management, him being bereaved and all. We can make a powerful lot of improvements in a week." I brightened up, just thinking about it.

"Meg, you are an impossible optimist."

"Nope, just like to make the best of what's set in front of me. The Lord said, 'As you sow, so shall you reap.' Seems to me that the Lord just naturally brought us here to see how we could improve Joe Scraggs's life. Might be needing similar help ourselves someday." Then I squared my shoulders. "Let's make a foray about the place, see what really needs tending to most."

Once Johnny saw that my mind was most definitely made up, he put his back into the job as well. The week passed in a flurry of activity. We tended to the animals, removed the manure piles from the vicinity of the cabin and spread them over the fields and buried the garbage. I settled down to butter and cheese making. Day before I expected him back, I did up a batch of fresh loaves to welcome Joe Scraggs and his bride. When we were tired, we sat in front of the cabin and tried to play his instruments. I was beginning to get the hang of the banjo, and didn't I just relish it. Never could understand my Pa's aversion to a little joyful music. Seemed to me you could praise the Lord that way just as easy as with a downcast countenance. A lot more cheerful, too. On the seventh day after Scraggs' departure, Johnny got a bad case of the jitters. Put me in mind of what might happen if he really were forced to settle down on one plot of ground. His feet were made for traveling, for sure. Lucky thing there was still a lot of ground to cover in this country. I just ignored his state of mind and made up a nice pot of soup out of a big hambone and some dried peas I'd found. Had to admit I *was* enjoying playing house with my own hearth and all. Especially since I'd cleaned it to my specifications.

'Round about supper time I heard a horse coming through the woods. True to his promise, Scraggs had returned. Anxious to find what he'd picked, I rushed out to see. Sitting astride the saddle behind him was a big, buxom blond girl, with a guitar slung over her shoulder. Johnny ran out from the barn and we both gave them big smiles, Johnny's definitely tinged with relief.

Joe Scraggs got off his horse and helped the girl down.

"Meet my wife Ingrid. Straight off the boat from Germany, she is. Don't seem to speak no English, but she plays her guitar like an angel. Found her down by the wharf, sitting on her small pile of clothes and wonderin' what to do. Picked her up right smart before they took her off to the city poor house. Lucky there was someone nearby to interpret for us, 'cause she came willingly to the first church to exchange vows."

Ingrid beamed, and I let out a sigh of relief. Obviously this would be a marriage made in heaven. I showed her into the cabin, pointing out the high points of her new domain. She nodded and smiled at everything. Then I fed them all. That night we had a high old musical time. Joe Scraggs gave me pointers on my banjo technique, and if there were any last bugs or sad spirits left in that house, well, we just chased them right out. The next morning Johnny and I set off with the sun for Cincinnati with an empty wagon and a purse full of gold coins. Not to mention my banjo.

We both felt kind of carefree, and the horse seemed to sense it as well, or maybe he was just trotting along faster because he had less load to pull. When we stopped for lunch Johnny finally counted out the money. He looked up from his labors with a smile.

"Seems to me we've got enough to cover new books, the wintering, and maybe even a secondhand printing press, if we can find someone willing to part with one."

I felt a little worried. "Seems a high price for a week's work on a farm. Sure we didn't take advantage of the man?"

"Now don't you go feeling sorry for Joe Scraggs, Meg. I believe he was a happy man as we parted. And you saw how Ingrid lit right into tending the house and the chickens this morning. There's no question in my mind that she came from a farm and knows a thing or two about caring for them. Also saw to it that he was left with some money, too. Wanted to give me the whole bag, he did, before I protested."

"Well, in that case . . ." And I smiled as he let me fondle the twenty-dollar gold pieces. Never had seen that much hard cash before.

"I figure we've got about two hundred dollars excess here, Meg. When we get into Cincinnati our first stop will be The Cincinnati Type Foundry Company. We'll look over their wares and see how far this will go."

So we had a light dinner of bread and cheese and set off again into the beautifully crisp afternoon, munching apples.

CHAPTER 9

Wasn't till just about noon the next day that we finally arrived in Cincinnati. I knew we had to be close when we began to be crowded off the road by droves of pigs being herded in to the slaughter houses. Thousands of them, there were, and it didn't look like any fun being one of the drovers, either. Pigs definitely have minds of their own.

Johnny said we'd be rid of them soon, and sure enough, just at the outskirts of the city, they were headed off to the west, to a place Johnny called "The Valley of Desolation." Said he walked out there once, just once last winter, and never would forget the sights and smells. Used to be called Deer Creek, but there sure weren't any deer left, just a dark red stream they dumped the blood and guts into. Can't say I had a yen to head that way too soon.

We drove the wagon south into the city proper. My, what a place! Even had some macadamed roads, though the gravel was sinking down into the mud from the heavy rains several weeks before. We came in from the northeast and followed the little canal down through the German section of the city. Johnny said the canal had been nicknamed "The Rhine" for a famous river in Germany in Old Europe, and its occupants call this neighborhood of the city "Over the Rhine."

Before we knew it, we were at the Fifth Street Market. Never saw so many human beings in my life. Had to step down from the wagon and lead Dickens to keep him from getting upset in all the confusion. Must've been over four hundred wagons set out, with their owners huckstering their goods—everything from fruit to meat to cages full of wild pigeons. I just stared and stared, and tried to keep out of the way of the wild hogs that clustered everywhere, ready to snatch and gobble fallen bits of produce. Acted just like our hounds back home, they did. Even saw some youngsters riding the bigger ones, at least for a piece until they were shaken off onto the street. Little ragamuffins they were, not much bigger than Charlie, and looking mighty pleased with their exploits. Took awhile for Johnny to drag me away from that spectacle, especially since it went on for about fifteen blocks, ending with a big horse market where farmers were showing off the finer points of their animals.

Then we were walking Dickens and the wagon through a fine piece of town. Beautiful red brick houses, with shiny white shutters we saw, and occasionally a fine lady stepping down to enter a fancy carriage. Some houses—more like my idea of mansions, really—had their fronts all covered with fine stone, too. It was late afternoon and I was still a little stupefied at all the marvels around us when Johnny finally got us to something he called the "industrial" part of town. He led the horse and wagon into the courtyard of the foundry company he'd been talking about, then left me with Dickens and Felicity while he went in to look over their goods. I waited a long while, then walked around the block to try to trace the columns of black smoke I saw spouting everywhere. From the signs I read they seemed to be making everything from steamships (whatever they were) to reapers in this part of town. After I got back it was another little while before Johnny reappeared, waving some broadsheets in his hand. He hurried over to show me.

"Look here, Meg!" He was excited, practically shouting. "They've got the most amazing things in there. All kind of hand presses, perfect for our size, a little heavy though. And they're making the latest things, like Hoe's Washington Press, which is a wonder for sure." He calmed down some and poked a broadsheet under my nose. I looked at a picture of a fancy contraption, then read the fine print below.

> They are elegant in appearance; simple, quick, and powerful in operation; and combine every facility for the production of superior printing.

Then I looked at the price list. "Says here the cheapest is two hundred dollars plus ten dollars extra 'if the frame is made to be taken to pieces,' which ours will have to be. Plus three dollars for boxing. Looks to me like we're already thirteen dollars over budget, and that's not even taking into account buying some type so the thing'll have some use. And look here, Johnny, it says it weighs 710 pounds. How in the world do you figure Dickens to pull that and all the rest of us? And where will we put it anyhow? Wagon just barely holds us, now." I stopped to catch a crestfallen look on Johnny's face. I already'd figured out that although he was mighty high on ideas, practicality wasn't his strong point. Sure didn't mean to crush his hopes, but one of us had to be responsible for these fine details.

He shoved a lock of hair out of his eyes and took on a determined look. "We'll work it out, Meg; we'll work it out." He took up Dicken's harness and started in to lead him out. "Come on. Let's find a place to camp for the night."

He led us then down to the banks of the Ohio. The light was going fast, but I managed to glimpse a fine big ship at the wharf, with a kind of a huge wheel just sticking up from it.

"What in the world is that?"

"Something, isn't it? It's a steamboat with a paddlewheel. Got lots of them here. They do trade all the way down to New Orleans, and up as far as St. Paul. Got engines inside that push the big wheel so it can go upstream, against the current."

"Really?" I asked in awe. I took another look at the huge thing, sort of like a sleeping mountain, maybe, was the closest I could come to describing it.

"Tell you what, Meg. Tomorrow we'll come and watch it start up and move out on the river, all right?"

"Yes!"

He had a hard time pulling me away, but soon we were moving on, looking for a piece of free ground with some grass, so we could take Dickens out of harness for the night. Not much grass, no matter how you looked at it. Johnny had said that we'd have to put the horse in a stable for board while we were in the city, but I was only now beginning to realize the need of it. Who'd think there could be a place with so many buildings, so close together like this city? Of course, I'd read lots of books about cities, but somehow they'd always seemed like fairy tales, with me tucked away out on the farm like that. Sure were a lot of wonders in God's world.

When I awoke the next morning, Johnny was already out and gone. Figured he'd be back soon hungry, so I lit up the Franklin stove with our small supply of wood and made up a mess of porridge. There was a nip in the air this morning and it would go down real nice. Felicity liked it too, which was a

128

constant amazement to me. I watched her clean up her plate, then set about braiding my hair and getting dressed.

When I finally stepped out of the wagon, I met a powerful sight. The sun was coming up over the eastern length of the river, setting rosy red glints all down the water. I stopped right then and there and let off a few prayers of thanksgiving for the glories of the Lord's world.

I was still feeling mighty fine about it all the whole time I was currying Dickens and feeding him some oats. A pleasing-looking chestnut, he was, and young and strong, too. He seemed to like the smell of the river and kept whinnying toward it, as if he wanted a closer look. I'd just finished all the chores and was wondering what to do next when I heard Johnny's whistle coming close. In another minute he was around the wagon, his hands full of buckets and paper.

"Look here, Meg!" He set down the buckets and handed me a copy of *The Cincinnati Daily Gazette*.

"What's all this? You never mean shops are open and it not even half past six yet?"

"Cincinnati's a forward-looking city, Meg. Most folks have their shops open by five in the morning. Usually take a couple of hours break by nine. But look here!" And he pointed to the front page of the newspaper, filled with advertisements.

"Exactly where, Johnny?"

He stabbed his finger at an already worn spot and I read the fine print.

Printer's devil wanted at *Gazette* office. Applicants to apply at noon today.

"There's our answer, Meg! We'll forego Chicago till next season, spend the winter here instead. I'll learn how to set type and run the presses, and earn a little extra money as well. Come spring, we'll be all organized!"

"What about me? What am I supposed to do the whole time you're working?" It must've come out as a wail, for Johnny just looked at me a minute.

"Hadn't thought about that. Suppose there's a lot of looking you can be doing, Meg. Learn about the city and its ways."

"I sure was looking forward to doing that with you."

He put his arm around my shoulder then and sweet-talked me some. Guess he figured that would make up for his getting his way. Well, it did help. Knew he'd get his way anyhow. Men always did. And he did need to get some training in this printing business. I sighed.

"All right, Johnny. And good luck to you in getting the job." I ran my fingers over his bristly face. "It's a shave you'll be needing, and a wash, and see that you put on your best shirt and frock coat. Appearances are important."

"Yes, ma'am. But that'll wait for a bit. Have another little project for the morning." He went to the buckets and pulled a wide brush and a thin one out of his back pocket. I watched him as he opened the first bucket.

"A little unfinished business," was all he said as he dipped the brush in the whitewash and carefully began to paint over the wagon side where it said "Chas. Stuart and Son, Booksellers." Then he opened the second bucket. Red paint, it was. He carefully began lettering in "John and Margaret Stuart, Booksellers."

"Oh, Johnny!" He certainly did know how to cheer me up when the occasion was warranted.

He knew I was pleased when I picked up the spare brush and began systematically to whitewash the rest of the wagon. Heaven knows it was overdue by several years now. I was still at it when he went in for

130

his breakfast, then began to get ready for the job interview.

When he left, all shiny and handsome in his wedding shirt, I asked him to bring back little buckets of blue and green and yellow as well. Might as well do up the wagon proper.

It was near sunset and I was finishing up the red roof when Johnny finally got back, looking like a cat that swallowed the mouse. I clambered down and stood there.

"Well?"

"There were forty men lined up for that job, Meg, some of them with true experience at type casting."

"Yes?"

"Well, seems none of them could spell worth a plugged nickel. I got the job!"

"That's wonderful, Johnny!" And I almost gave him a huge hug, but remembered the paint all over me just in time.

"Tell me about it!"

"It's ten to twelve hours a day, depending on the need, six days a week. Get paid each Saturday—four dollars."

"Is that good?"

"Well, I figure that for five months' work it's good for about eighty dollars. Jacob Young was telling me that circuit riders get sixty-four dollars for a whole year's work, and they have a time collecting it. With our wintering money in hand, it should be free and clear, maybe enough for the type."

"When do you start?"

"Tomorrow morning at six."

"Oh."

"You'll have to do the book buying, Meg. That should keep you busy for a while."

"Think I'd like to whitewash the inside of the wagon, too."

"Good idea. Uhm. I forgot to get your paint, Meg."

"Never you mind. You'll have to give me directions and I'll go for it tomorrow. Maybe walk you to your job, if you'd like that."

"You know I would."

He was looking a little strained at deserting me like that, so I changed the subject to supper and went to try and get myself cleaned up some.

The next few weeks were a trial for me for sure. I spent my days painting that wagon inside and out till it shone. Even painted little flowers and animals around the outside and inside for some extra color. Finally there was just not an inch of wagon left to fuss over. Then I'd go down to the wharf and watch the boats coming and going. I listened in to the talk of the passengers and officers, too. Lots of talk there was about how one steamboat's engine was faster than another, and about the races they sometimes had on the river. 'Course there was some talk about accidents, too, about pushing the engines too hard and having them explode, killing passengers with scalding water and flying debris. Didn't seem to bother the customers none. Seemed like they were only interested in speed, and took on a kind of cavalier, devil-may-care attitude about the dangers involved. After that, I wasn't sure I really wanted to ride one of those steamboats anymore, but it still was interesting to watch.

Also spent some time watching the ferry boat come across the river from Kentucky. Saw my first black man getting off the boat one day and learned he was a slave come to shop for his master across the river. Handsome man he was, in an exotic kind of way. Put me in mind of Shakespeare's *Othello*.

That night I asked Johnny about the blacks and he explained to me about Kentucky's being a slave state and Ohio being a free one. Said lots of blacks came through across the river at night and were hidden in

132

something called "The Underground Railroad" that helped them to get up to Canada and a free life. He said the Beechers up at the Lane Theological Seminary on the hill above the city were whispered to be big abolitionists and a part of it all, but most of the city folks just turned a deaf ear and blind eye to the goings-on. To think all this was happening around me, and I never knew! Must say I couldn't blame the slaves any for wanting to be free. Not much point to life otherwise.

Would've spent more time at the waterfront, but some of the sailors coming off the boats were a rough lot, and I didn't want to be taken as an easy woman, having just found out what *they* were by hanging around there. Guess that was an education in itself. And it did seem a pity all those little shacks near the docks were filled with saloons. Poor sailors didn't have half a chance with all the temptations beckoning to them.

So I finally left the river, which I loved, and made a few tentative explorations inland. Found Main Street all right, and that kept me busy for a week or two. Must have been thirty or more bookstores all lined up in a row there. I carried our book money strapped down inside my blouse so I couldn't have my skirt pockets picked by any of the low-type ruffians that lounged about. Worse than Fagin, some of them looked, too.

I'd spend a few hours browsing, then when I'd made my choice, I'd have to go out to a privy in the back alley to free up the payment. Most of the booksellers were connected to printing shops and the clerks got to know me real well, as Johnny Stuart's wife. That pleased me, but even better it got me discount prices on the books. Nice to be considered one of the trade.

For our stock of *McGuffey's* I had to go to Johnny's printing plant, Morgan Lodge Fisher. Turned out their five presses printed not only *The Gazette*, but all the book work for Truman Smith, the *McGuffey's* publishers, as well. Made a nice discovery there which pleased me immensely, a new book for teaching numbers—*Ray's Arithmetics, First, Second, and Third Parts.* Seemed to me it would make a good companion piece for selling with our *McGuffey's* on the road. I took home a set, pleased as punch, to show Johnny, then started in to study from it myself. Johnny showed a mild interest from the sales point of view, but I guess he always would be more comfortable with words than numbers. He said as how all those figures looked worse than Greek to him.

Once, on a trip to his plant, I sneaked a look into the back room and saw Johnny there—at least his tall back, hunched over the type cases. Made the rest of my day, it did.

Johnny would head off first thing after breakfast and come home pale and exhausted, with mean inkstains all over his skin and clothes. And those stains just would not come off. Johnny just laughed over his "type-case hands." He said that any ink made of lampblack and oil was sure to have no end of staying power. He brought home his type stick and some lead slug letters to show me what he was doing. Said the hardest part was memorizing the locations of the letters in the type cases so that he could put together and break apart words and sentences as fast as possible. It seemed that putting out the *Daily Gazette* was just a small part of what he did. The big part was what he called "job-printing"—doing up advertising broadsheets for the different merchants around town. I didn't like how wan and thin he was getting from being indoors all the time, but there wasn't much I could do about it.

Way into the beginning of November we'd keep moving Dickens and the wagon farther and farther

134

around the outskirts of town, trying to keep the horse in grass as long as possible. Finally, when the snows started to come, there wasn't anything to do but board him up at a stable. I used to go and visit him each day to cheer him up, but I could tell Dickens was a lot like Johnny, and just needed to be out on the road again.

'Round about the same time, it got to be too cold for sleeping in the wagon as well, so I found us a boarding house in the German part of town. Mrs. Ziegler, our landlady, was a cheerful widow lady who was looking for an extra pair of hands, so I offered mine to help cover our expenses. She took me on for a day or two trial; decided I was well worth it, and agreed to halve our six-dollar-a-week charges for my labors. After that, it was a little easier. We put the wagon in the back yard and covered it with tarpaulins for the winter.

I had somebody to talk to, and even began to learn German from the landlady and all the other boarders. Never could tell when it might come in handy, especially in that part of town where everybody seemed to speak nothing but German. Even the shop signs were printed in German. It was easy to figure out that *backerei* meant *bakery*. And it was fun to go in and smell the fresh loaves piled up high. They had all sorts I'd never tasted, like pumpernickel and rye. Imagine not having to bake your own bread! Wouldn't Ma just get a thrill over it! *Spezerei-handlung* for *grocery store* was a little more complicated, but I mostly went down to the Fifth Street Market, anyhow, where there was more to be had and it was easier to bargain.

Mrs. Ziegler disliked going out into the cold to do the marketing, but I enjoyed it mightily, so I took on that chore as well. Gave me a chance at some fresh air, even though it was a fairish walk from the house on Vine Street. I always had a few minutes to browse in the bookstores and pick up a new or old volume or two for the wagon. Also picked up a little English-German dictionary for my use and took to studying it at odd moments.

I soon leaned that it wasn't that much harder cooking for twenty than for a hungry farm family of seven. Just more of everything. Mrs. Ziegler taught me to make all kinds of noodles, and I must say Johnny and I both took to this new addition to our meals. There was always some kind of a pot pie as well, with a thick crust of bread, baking golden on top. And endless sauerkraut, mashed potatoes, and spare ribs.

Turned out I got to know the slaughter houses better than I ever wanted to. They couldn't pack the ribs in their barrels of salt pork, so every day there were pounds and pounds of spare ribs, not to mention lights, free for the taking. And Mrs. Ziegler wasn't about to pass up that golden opportunity, especially after she had me to do the fetching. So once or twice a week I took Dickens out of his stable and rode him with a borrowed saddle and my baskets slung behind from ropes up along "Bloody run" to "The Valley of Desolation." Soon found out it was also called "Valley of the Shadow of Death," among other things.

We'd go along the Ohio to the point where the creek ran red into it—mighty close to the waterworks intake, it seemed to me—I never would drink any of the Cincinnati water after that. Then we'd go up the hill and I'd stand in line with my baskets, like lots of other womenfolk, many of them with babes hanging onto their skirts, looking frightened at the sounds and smells. Dickens wasn't crazy about the neighborhood, either. Animals kind of sense danger to their kind. But he did love to get out of that stable, and enjoyed the ride near the river. I'd be sitting astride him, bundled in my warm cloak, wishing Johnny were out with us, at least to feel the cold winter air on his face. Then, too soon, it would be time to return to the house and get on with the endless cleaning or the preparations for the next meal.

Amazing it was to watch the boarders set down to a meal. At home and on the road, mealtime was always the time of day to relax a little and talk over the events that had happened, kind of friendly-like. But these people weren't interested in anything but gulp and gobble. It would take us three hours to get the table heaped with food, and then it would be gone in ten minutes, everybody up and away to do whatever it was they did with the rest of their time.

They were polite, though, even at breakfast. Wasn't one of them wouldn't set down at the table with a "good morning," or "*guten tag*." Even had an Austrian who always started out with "*gruss gott*." Kind of liked that salutation. Nice to see somebody still keeping God foremost. Then they'd really tuck into the coffee and tea, ham and eggs, roasted chickens, salad, pickles, vinegar, pepper, hot biscuits, buckwheat cakes, and butter. Even straight off the farm I couldn't keep up with that kind of eating. Tried it once and had indigestion till noon. Johnny and I just kind of settled on the ham and eggs and biscuits and let it be at that.

Sometimes on a Saturday evening, though, they'd all gather in the downstairs parlor and Johnny and I would bring out the concertina and banjo. The prim schoolteacher who lived with us played cello and she'd haul it out as well. A big, bullet-headed man by the name of Juergen—he was setting up a little candle and soap factory—emerged after a few Saturdays, almost shyly, with a violin, and began to join us. And sometimes Mrs. Ziegler would sit down at her parlor organ and play as well. None of us talked much during these occasions. Just agreed on a tune, then tried to figure out how to get our instruments in tune with the others.

One day, just before Christmas, a music master came to stay. George Mueller was horrified at our lack of formal instruction, and decided to enlighten us. He started in with lectures on how to read notes and all. Can't say I minded the instruction, but I did notice that the spontaneity of the events disappeared rather suddenly. He kept casting black looks at my banjo, referring to it as an ungodly, uncivilized instrument. Got me good and fed up, he did, to the point that I finally asked him if he had a better suggestion. Apparently he did, for a few days later he presented my with a little wooden flute-like thing that he called a "sopranino recorder." Said it was about time we added a wind instrument to the *ensemble*. Well, I didn't care much for his attitude, but the sounds from that little thing were sweet as a bird's song, so I went along with it to please him.

It was two days before Christmas, a Saturday morning, and I had just finished sweeping off the front steps and giving them their Saturday-morning whitewash. Mrs. Ziegler and all her German neighbors, no matter the weather, whitewashed their front steps each and every Saturday morning. Gave the brick row houses a nice, bright appearance, and I could tell, come summer, when all those flowerpots on the front windows were filled with geraniums, the houses would look spritely. I was sent out hunting for a few really plump geese and turkeys for the festivities. Heard that turkeys had gone up to twenty-five cents apiece and I was concentrating on how to bargain the hucksters down some as I walked over to the market.

There I was slogging along through the snow and mud, trying to keep my skirts moderately clean, and was almost to the market when I heard a pitiful crying coming from one of the sheds along the alley. I almost walked past, then it started up again and I just had to go and see what the problem was. I poked open a tumbledown door, empty baskets first to give myself some measure of protection just in case it was some riff-raff off the river looking to trick a passerby. (I'd learned a thing or two about city life in these months, I had.) I peered in and it took me a moment or two to adjust my eyes to the darkness. Then I gave a little gasp.

Curled up on a bed of filthy straw was the scrawniest youngster I'd ever seen, just bawling his heart out. I went over for a closer look. He stopped crying for a moment, but started in again when I tried to touch him. Didn't look more than four years of age, and he was dressed in the sorriest rags. Couldn't be doing much to keep off the cold. Well, I just laid down my baskets and took that child in my arms.

"What's the matter, honey? Where are your mama and papa? Where is your home?"

He paused in the middle of a wail. "Sick. Deaded." And he let in to snuffling again.

And that's all I could get out of him. So I picked him up and continued on to the market. I asked around some and found he'd been stealing food worse than the hogs last few weeks. Everybody had seen him, but nobody had given him a second glance, except to maybe give him a good thrashing and send him off again. By this time, the fellow was walking next to me, holding my hand for dear life, maybe figuring I'd protect him from another thrashing. I looked at him again. Nothing on his feet. They were bloody and blue from the cold. I sighed.

"What's your name?"

Sniff. "Jamie." Sniff.

That was the final straw. Had my own Pa's name. Brought on a wave of homesickness like I couldn't remember.

"Come on, Jamie. We'll just buy our geese and turkeys and you'll come home with me." He didn't particularly brighten up at that, but then he didn't let go of my hand, either.

On the way back we stopped at a cobbler's and a haberdashery store and I had him measured up for some boots and a pair of trousers, two shirts, and a warm winter jacket. Then I bought some wool for socks and a muffler and mittens. I could start in knitting tonight. Time I had something to do with my hands again anyway. The money would just have to come out of the printing press. Wasn't any other choice. With the merchants' promise to have them ready for the next day, I took Jamie home to Mrs. Ziegler. Should've expected her response.

"*Gott in himmel!* I send you out for geese and you bring home a street urchin!"

"Now, Mrs. Ziegler, it is Christmas. I'm just calling Jamie here an early present."

"And who pays for his room and board?"

"He can bunk down with Johnny and me, and I'll pay for his meals. He can't eat more than a dollar's worth a week, can he? He's only a small child."

She looked at me. "We will see what he eats. And your Johnny needs some privacy with you. He works hard and deserves that much. Hardly married, you are. The boy we'll put up in the attic. No charge."

I smiled. "Thank you, Mrs. Ziegler."

She looked at him again. "Get out the washtub. Bugs I don't need in my clean house. It is hard enough to keep the dust out."

I grinned to myself and got to work. Before you knew it Mrs. Ziegler was down on her knees next to me, scrubbing with a will. Had to cut off most of Jamie's hair, but when we were finished he wasn't all that bad to look at. Wasn't till we had him dressed in Johnny's spare work shirt that we remembered the inner child as well and offered him something to eat. Nothing wrong with him that a month or two of Mrs. Zielger's noodles wouldn't cure.

Felicity had been watching all this activity with interest from her warm spot by the fire. When we had Jamie presentable and fed, she lazily got up, stretched, and ambled over to give him a sniff. Apparently she approved, for she stretched up and gave his face a long wet lick with her tongue. This elicited the boy's first smile, and for the rest of the long afternoon the two of them frolicked together on the floor amongst our busy feet as we made supper preparations. Kind of nice having a youngster underfoot again. Almost had me in tears thinking of Charlie and young Sarah back home.

Just before supper, Johnny came in from work through the kitchen door. He knew Mrs. Ziegler was always fussing around the dining room at that time and it gave us a minute alone together. One of my favorite moments of the day, it was, to rush into his arms for a good hug and kiss, and know he'd really missed me and loved me. Today, however, I was dreading the moment a little. How would he react to Jamie? Should've known better. Jamie was hanging by my skirts, practically calling me "Mama" when Johnny burst in the door. Johnny stopped, arms spread wide. Slowly his arms dropped down to his side.

"Was wondering how long it would take you to pick up another orphan, Meg." He lowered himself to his knees and gave the boy a good look. Then he smiled. "What's your name, son?"

"Jamie."

Johnny looked at me again. "Guess some things are just ordained."

"Is it all right, Johnny? He was so hungry and alone and it's Christmas soon. . . ."

"I guess the Lord will provide."

And then I got my kiss. A right proper one it was, too.

Mr. Juergen came home hauling a huge spruce tree. Everybody lit up at the *tannenbaum* and we spent a festive evening decorating it. Even Mr. Mueller loosened up and taught us some German Christmas songs to sing and play on our instruments afterward. Little Jamie was exhausted, but his wide eyes would not close, so I let him snuggle next to me on the rug as I busily knit a pair of socks for his feet.

Finally he fell asleep and Johnny carried him up to the bed Mrs. Ziegler and I had prepared for him in the attic. I followed, fussing like a mother hen, Johnny claimed. Reminded me of the loft back home when I was a child, with the bits and pieces of things tucked about and the smells from the smoked meats and a few herbs stored there. Before I knew it, I was crying like a baby and Johnny was carrying me down to our room where he gently deposited me on the big soft bed.

"What's the matter, Meg, love? Missing your family?"

"Oh, Johnny! Yes!"

He snuggled down next to me and cuddled me. "I've been thinking. Come spring, what's to keep us from heading down to the farm and visiting a bit before going on to Chicago? It's not much of a trip, and we could even stop by the Scraggses and see how Joe has managed with his Ingrid."

"Johnny! Could we?"

"Can't see any reason not to." He thought some more. "Why don't you write a letter to your folks? Mail's getting pretty good these days. Make you feel better, like you're talking to them."

I sat up then. "Of course, you're right, Johnny. Never though about the writing because I never did it before. And we never did get any letters at home." I started feeling excited. "First thing tomorrow morning, after the breakfast is cleared up, when the lunch is on its way. . . ."

142

He smiled. "Just have to think things out to feel better, Meg. Tell them about young Jamie. Seems to me he might have an easier time growing up on the farm than traveling around with us. Your pa can always use an extra hand."

I frowned. "Getting attached to the boy already. We'll have to wait and see about that."

"All right. But now I mean to direct your mind away from all that." And he began to unbraid my hair, the way he liked to at night. I sighed happily.

Christmas Day finally came and it was lovely. I surprised Johnny with a recent book by Washington Irving, *The Adventures of Captain Bonneville U.S.A. in the Rocky Mountains and the Far West*. He presented me with James Fenimore Cooper's *Pathfinder*, with a few words about Cooper being the new American Scott, definitely a writer to watch. And there was a set of lovely combs for my hair. Jamie got his new clothes and walked around, proud as a peacock in his new finery. The boy took to Johnny right off and was soon calling him "Pa" and me "Ma." Felt kind of funny being called that. I was beginning to understand the responsibility attached. Couldn't chide him into calling us anything else, though. He just did what came naturally. That boy just crawled all over Johnny, and soon Johnny was casting off his self-consciousness and enjoying it as well. Maybe since he'd been a kind of half-orphan, he could understand the need more than some. The German boarders were loath to get involved at first, but gradually Jamie's smiles began to warm them up, too.

I sure hated to let Johnny head off to work again after having him around for two whole days between Sunday and Christmas, but there wasn't anything to be done about it. Spring would be coming in a few months and we would be free again. Sure was looking forward to spring. But first we had to get into the new year. 1844. Sounded nice to me.

Seems like in Cincinnati they celebrated the coming of the year with some hoopla. Christmas was just past when Mrs. Ziegler and I began baking cakes for the next round of festivities. New Year's Day after breakfast we set the dining room table full of sweet things, and then the door knocker started in to pounding. Went on for hours, into the night, old friends coming to call. Had a big bowl filled with punch and a keg of beer for the offering. Johnny and I didn't touch the spirits, but the Germans did, and smiled a lot more than usual. I was good and tired, though, by the end of the day, what with trying to keep Jamie out of the cakes and pies. It would be nice to hear a house full of English again, too.

January was a little more tranquil, except for the snow followed by rain. Rained so bad, I read in Johnny's *Gazette* that one night a stranger to the city had fallen into an open cellar and drowned while walking down Broadway. Took till noon to haul him out. Funny things happened in cities. Mrs. Ziegler used to talk about the cholera epidemic of '37 and shiver at the thought of its maybe coming again some summer. I shivered too and knew I wouldn't be found in any city come midsummer. Smoke and grime and garbage of Cincinnati was bad enough in winter. Johnny's Oregon Trail was looking more pleasing all the time. Not that either of us knew for sure what we'd do once we actually arrived there. Just to be talking about the *going* seemed enough for the moment, especially for Johnny.

Toward the end of January I just started in praying for the spring to come earlier than ever. Johnny had added a nasty cough to his wanness, and overall he just began to look downright consumptive. But he refused to take time off from the job to get better. Said there was still to much for him to learn, and not that much time left in the winter for the learning. If it hadn't been for being tied down with Mrs. Ziegler's boarding house and now Jamie, I would've tried getting myself a job at a bindery. That way, one of us would know that end of the printing business.

Come February, Mrs. Ziegler started in complaining. However would she manage the place after Johnny and I had gone with the spring? I appreciated the thought, but figured she could get herself a good maidservant straight off the boat from Germany pretty fast.

Took to spending my free time, such as it was, starting in Jamie with reading and numbers. He was quick for sure, and especially loved his numbers. He'd count out the silverware as he helped to set the table each mealtime, and even learned subtraction by counting up all the firewood in the kitchen, then throwing logs into the fire one by one and figuring how much was left.

Once I'd started in with my letters home, I began writing each week. I guess it was almost like keeping a journal in a way, telling them about the funny things the boarders did—like Mr. Juergen's love of what he called "physical culture." Five nights a week he'd go off to his physical culture club to do heaven knows what, and come home sweating and steaming. Even took to showing Jamie how to do headstands and somersaults on the parlor floor. In a gruff sort of way, he seemed to enjoy the child. Mr. Juergen had also begun casting long glances at our spinster schoolteacher, Miss Mecklenberg, who must've been well into her thirties. She didn't seem to mind none, and when he actually began to forego his evening visit to his club to escort her to a series of lectures on astronomy at the museum, I figured there might be a wedding come spring or summer.

Well, for about two months I'd been sort of casting all these missives to my family off into the blue, so to speak, never expecting any reply. A shock it was, then, when one day about the middle of February the postman comes to the door. He left a few letters from Germany for assorted boarders. But at the bottom of the pile was one addressed to me! Mrs. Margaret Stuart! First I was thrilled, then I just sort of stared at it, getting scared. Had to be from home—that was Pa's tentative hand for sure. I picked it up gingerly and walked it into the kitchen to show Mrs. Ziegler.

"Gott in himmel!" (That was her favorite expression when riled or excited.) "Open it, child! Never will you know the inside from just staring at the outside!"

So I opened it. Recognized at once the endpaper from one of my books. Have to be taking them a ream of writing paper for sure on our visit if I didn't expect the whole family library to be destroyed. Looked short enough. How much bad news could you tell in such a short space? Finally let my eyes focus on the words:

To our dear daughter and her husband,

Your ma and I and the young ones thank you for your letters. Never expected a single one, but after they started coming we enjoyed them to no end. We are all fine, aside from the usual winter ills. We look forward to your spring visit and will keep the boy, Jamie, if it suits everyone. I hope you are reading your Bible each day and keeping close to the Lord, like you were brung up.

Your father,
James McDonald

Well, I sat down then at the kitchen table and had a good cry. Jamie brought me a rag to blow my nose and Mrs. Ziegler kept asking what was wrong. Finally got myself together enough to say that everything was just fine. Just fine. She beamed.

"So why the tears then, *liebchen*? Dry your eyes and thank the good God for your fortune. Your husband, he comes soon. To upset him, you don't want.''

I followed her orders, shooed Jamie from my lap, and went to check on the ham roasting over the fire.

Before I knew it, it was mid-March and the freeze was letting up. Carefully I unwrapped the wagon and cleaned and aired it and all of our belongings. Our clothes had been carefully mended and readied as well. Johnny still had his cough, but was acting more cheerful now that spring was almost upon us.

One day we sat down and counted our money. It was soon apparent that even with both of us working all winter, there still wasn't enough for the press and the type. Johnny decided on a compromise. We'd spend the money on a good set of type here in Cincinnati where it was made and could be gotten easily. It didn't weigh that much and we could cart it with us until we had enough laid by for the press. So that's what we did.

Johnny constructed a kind of holding space under the wagon, bought his type, and carefully packed it up for the duration. This done, he was ready to leave and we only waited until the rains had let up for a week and the roads outside the city would be passable again.

One fine day at the end of March we picked up Dickens, harnessed him up, packed our belongings in the wagon and stowed Jamie on the seat up front. Mrs. Ziegler gave us enough food for an army and stood waving us off from her front stoop, a few tears in her eyes. I smiled back and we all waved from our vantage point on the wagon. We were all excited. We were going on the road again.

CHAPTER 10

It was a spritely day for sure. Tiny buds were starting to green up on some of the earlier trees and the birds were singing for all they were worth.

The three of us were singing, too, once we got past the outskirts of Cincinnati. I started in with a rousing version of "Onward, Christian Soldiers," and soon Johnny and Jamie were chiming in. Felt like a holiday for all of us.

Already, Johnny was looking healthier, and Jamie had fattened up real nice in the months with Mrs. Ziegler. He was a bright little boy, always asking questions. And Johnny and I were always willing to answer them. We'd been talking about Ma and Pa's farm to him, and he was excited to see it. Of course we didn't say naught about leaving him there. Have to wait and see how he took to it and everyone.

We had made some attempts at trying to locate his original family. Johnny had checked with the orphanages in the city, and with the police. Even with the riders that came around now and again searching for lost children. We had finally given up on it, and I was glad. Whoever his parents had been (and he never seemed able to remember much about them), they had bred a decent and clever little boy. A good growing-up should take care of the rest of him.

After we'd stopped for our midday meal, I dug out my little sopranino recorder. Mr. Mueller had given it to me for keeps the night before we left. He'd been as nice about it as he could in his pompous way, humphing and grumphing and muttering in German something abut my having natural talent for it and music in general. So I spent the afternoon imitating bird calls that we'd hear along the pike, then passing it over to Jamie and letting him have a go at it. He hadn't quite gotten down the "breath control," as Mr. Mueller called it, but he was trying mightily. Sure was pleasant having a ready-made youngster along with us to brighten the day. While Johnny and I hadn't produced one of our own yet, I didn't worry about it none. I figured I had a few good years left yet, and the Lord would take care of us when the time was ripe.

So we continued on our way into the afternoon until Johnny spotted a farmhouse he figured was far enough from the city for the occupants to possibly be interested in books. I could tell he was itching to try his hand at the selling again, so we pulled into the farmyard and waited for our customers to appear.

When a middle-aged farmer and his wife came out, we went through our little introductions, this time Johnny including Jamie as well. Jamie was pleased as punch and aped Johnny's bow to a T, down to the doffing of his hat. 'Course Jamie didn't have a hat yet, but that didn't bother him much. A natural-born actor, that one. He just pulled off an imaginary one and then swung it around in his hand, lifelike.

This little maneuver evoked great smiles from the lady of the house, and soon Jamie was sitting with me in the kitchen, eating great quantities of gingerbread cookies and downing an entire pint of fresh cow's milk. I was real pleased to see him taking to the milk like that. Couldn't get any for him in the city. It was sold there, of course, but there'd been so few cows in and around those parts that what milk was sold was watered down something fierce. Wouldn't give him that, especially since I'd heard that they fed the poor beasts on slop from the breweries. Didn't strike me as being healthy, somehow.

Well, the Missus and I got to talking about this and that—mainly how the wintering had been in the city—and she was soon telling me about her grown children, all gone farther west. Then she stopped for a moment, thinking. In a minute she'd gone off to another room to return with a little child's hat, a bit old and musty, but real close in looks to Johnny's broad-brimmed one.

She looked at me. "May I give it to your boy? It was my son's, him that's off in the Dakota Territory somewhere. Always thinking I'd have a grandchild to give it to someday, but if I have got one, I'm not knowing about it yet, and not likely to see the child in my lifetime."

Jamie stared at the hat, eyes gleaming, crumbs stuck to his open mouth.

"Would you like to have it, Jamie?" I asked, unnecessarily, of course.

"Yes, Mama! It's just like Pa's!"

"Thank you, ma'am. I'm thinking it will be properly appreciated."

To prove my point, Jamie left the last crumbs before him, then went to the woman and gingerly received the gift. Then he placed it on his head, just getting the feel. Finally, he backed away, and removed it with a flourish and a little bow.

"Thank you, ma'am. I will think of you each day it is upon my head, and thank the good Lord for your kindness."

Well, we both were a little taken aback by his fine

speech. Then he turned into a little boy again and went roaring out the door to show off the new hat to Johnny.

The woman looked at me. "I envy you your fine child, Mrs. Stuart. May the Lord bless you with more like him."

Well, there wasn't much I could add to that, so I just shut my mouth and smiled.

We left shortly thereafter, Johnny having sold the farmer a copy of Irving's *Captain Bonneville* so he could get an idea what his sons were up against on their travels. After Johnny and I had both read his Christmas copy, we'd stocked up on a few more, thinking the interest might be there. And it was. It chilled down some that night, and we had to light up the little stove to keep the freeze off while we were sleeping. I'd made a little mattress for Jamie that just fit into the floor space of the wagon at night. It was a bit cramped, but cozy, and the boy was so tired out after his first day on the road that he was in a deep sleep almost before I had him tucked in.

Johnny and I sat on the top bunk, looking at him and talking a bit before we slept ourselves. I told Johnny about Jamie's hat speech back at the farm.

"The boy has a good mind and a quick tongue," he smiled. "Already he's read through *McGuffey's Primer*. Can't remember if I was reading or not at that age." He looked down again at the little curled up figure, lank brown hair spread over the sheets. "He travels well, too. And always willing to help. It's a mighty temptation to hang on to him and see how he grows. Don't know that he's got the same frame of mind as your brothers, although I'll admit there's a lot to be learned on a farm, as well."

I looked at Jamie. "He's closest in age to Charlie. Charlie's quick like he is, too, not like Abe and Aaron. Born farmers they are, like my pa. I hate to say it, Johnny, but I don't know if I can leave him."

"Let's not worry about it any more tonight, Meg. Maybe we'll just leave it to Jamie to make up his mind after a few days on the farm."

With that, Johnny blew out the lantern.

Two days later we pulled into the Scraggses' farm. Wasn't sure at first we had the right place; it looked that different. The barn had been painted, new pens set up for the animals farther away from the cabin, and a little kitchen garden plowed and readied for planting. The cabin itself was in the throes of a new addition, as yet unfinished. The walls were almost up to roof level. We sat and stared some until Ingrid came to the door. Her face lit up like the sun when she saw us, and she started in yelling for Joe. Ingrid had changed, too. She was still as big and buxom as before, maybe more so. But she was leading heavily with her stomach as she came out the door.

I jumped off the wagon and got a good hug.

She pointed to her stomach. "Baby!" she beamed. "Joe's baby and Ingrid's!"

I tried out some of my German on her then. She just stared in awe for a moment, then let off almost faster that I could follow. Luckily Joe came up then, leading his horse and plow from the fields. He was grimy, but it was good clean dirt. His hair had grown out nicely, and he was sporting a big moustache and sideburns. He gave Johnny a back thumping that almost staggered my husband, then carefully washed his hands in the basin in front of the cabin before nearly shaking my hand off. Then they both spotted Jamie, and it was time for more introductions and explanations.

We had a nice dinner together in the spotlessly clean cabin, then Johnny went out into the fields to give Joe a hand, with Jamie tagging along. I puttered in the kitchen with Ingrid, helping her put together a festive supper and gossiping in a combination of German and English. She was interested in my city

152

experiences, but didn't seem to miss having the opportunity to live there. She was a good, basic, down-to-earth woman, delighted with her life with Joe. "Good man, my Joe," she continually reminded me with a smile.

After the supper and the Bible reading, we all got out our instruments. Joe was intrigued with the recorder, never having seen one before. 'Course he had to try it, but I can say without pride that I do believe stringed instruments were more in his line. He also approved of my improvements on the banjo. Jamie sat contentedly and listened to the music until Joe took down a small violin from the wall and gave him a few lessons. He explained that it was a "three-quarter" violin, and he hoped to be teaching his son how to play it someday very soon. 'Course then he had to stop and pat Ingrid's stomach lovingly. If it weren't for Jamie, I'd have felt mighty left out. Ingrid had let me touch her stomach earlier in the day and I'd felt the baby kicking with a will. Sure felt good. I just knew it would be a strapping big baby when it showed up in a few months.

Well, we played and talked till way after midnight, and the lot of us struggled up well past daybreak the next morning. Then it was time for us to be moving on. We all hugged considerable.

"My house is your house," Ingrid said with some effort as we climbed the wagon.

"Thank you, Ingrid," I smiled, and we clattered down the road.

Three days later we pulled into my old home. It had gotten colder the last day and an early spring snow-storm looked more than likely by the color of the late afternoon sky. It was funny coming around that bend through the trees and seeing the spread open up before us. Funny doing it from the opposite direction for a change. Then my ma came out the door, and

153

little Sarah reached up to pull the bell rope to call in Pa and the boys. My throat kind of choked up and before you knew it I was in my ma's arms, tears of happiness streaming down both our faces.

Suddenly I was surrounded by my brothers and a pack of hound dogs. Then my pa was shouldering his way through. I looked up.

"It's good to see you, daughter."

"Thank you, Pa." Then he got a great hug from me, too. He colored a little, but didn't push me away.

Finally I remembered Johnny and Jamie. I turned around. Ma was giving Johnny's coloring a good look—the kind of look she used to give his father when he started coming here poorly.

"Shame on you, Maggie. Have you been mistreating your man?"

"Don't you be picking on my wife, Ma McDonald. She tried her best to keep me out of the print shop all winter."

Then Ma looked down. "This must be your Jamie."

The boys had already been sizing up Jamie, but now he came into his own.

"Yes, ma'am, Jamie Stuart at your service." And he swung off his hat and made a magnificent bow.

Ma just looked for a moment, then wrapped him in her arms. "You are a fine wee one, for sure. Welcome to our home, Jamie. And praise the Lord for putting you in our Maggie's care. Couldn't find you a better mama."

"Yes, ma'am. I know that for sure," he agreed very solemnly.

Then little Sarah with her bright red hair walked right over to Jamie and gave him a hug. He smiled.

"Got hair like my mama, she has." He looked around. "Most all of you do. I like it fine. Wished I had some myself."

Well, that got all of us past the awkward stage and soon we were all smiling and helping to unload the wagon. I lined up the presents I'd brought from Cincinnati on the kitchen table. They'd cut into our profits considerably, but Johnny had never begrudged me the choosing or the spending. Had them all wrapped in old *Gazettes* and the youngsters were mighty curious. I started with Abe and Aaron first, handing them each a parcel long and thin.

"A little something invented by a man named Jim Bowie. A frontiersman and trapper, he was. Died in the Republic of Texas down South at the Alamo, fighting off the Mexicans—along with another famous frontiersman, Davy Crockett."

The boys had ripped off the paper before I'd finished my explanation, then stood in awe admiring their matching Bowie knives.

"Wow!" from Abe.

"This is a sharp 'un for sure!" from Aaron. "Thank you, Maggie."

"Hear as how they've been trying to get into the Union," Pa commented. "Texas, that is. Don't see how they're gonna manage it real soon with the competition on between new slave and free states."

"It is a problem at that, sir," spoke up Johnny.

And then the two of them were off on politics, like it used to be with Johnny's pa. I smiled and moved on to the next package while they dug into the rights and wrongs of the Missouri Compromise.

"This one's for little Sarah," I said.

Sarah held up her arms for the bulky package. Charlie gave her some help pulling off the paper. Soon a big doll was revealed. It had a real china head, painted with blond curls, and a soft kid body. Her dress was blue silk trimmed with cotton lace. Sarah's eyes opened and closed.

"Oh! She has drawers!" said Sarah, lifting the elegant skirt. "Beautiful dolly! Thank you, Mag!" And she promptly sat on the floor and began to croon and cuddle it.

Charlie was next, and he knew it. He stood waiting expectantly. I reached for the biggest package and he held his breath.

I gave him a hug and whispered in his ear, "Something special for you, Charlie." He tore into it. Then sat back and stared. It was a tiny printing press with a set of type, paper, and ink. It had set Johnny and me back a piece, but I figured that if we couldn't have one, somebody ought to, and Charlie struck me as the right one.

"Johnny and I will teach you how to use it, Charlie. You can print up your own books and stories with it."

His eyes gleamed and he started right in to pull the hand lever, and figure out how it worked. And Jamie was right beside him, fascinated. That left Ma and Pa. I reached for a long, heavy package and gave it to Pa. He stopped his conversation with Johnny to inspect it. The opening revealed a shining new saw and a set of chisels.

"Hope you have need of the tools, Pa. We thought they'd be some help with your ice harvesting and building.

He looked pleased as he examined the tools, then began to flex the saw blade.

"Thank you, Maggie. Had no need to be bringing presents at all. Yourself was enough. But I thank you." Then he went out back with a curious expression on his face, and in another minute I could hear him testing the new saw on a piece of wood.

I looked up at my mother and handed her the last present. "For you, Ma. Something pretty as you are to look upon."

She fumbled with the cord, then gently pushed aside the paper and padding of rags to reveal a porcelain statue of a beautiful fine lady dressed like some I'd seen in Cincinnati.

"It's real porcelain, Ma, from Staffordshire, England. I guess that would make her a real English lady.

156

They have things like that in Cincinnati. I wanted you to know.''

She carefully picked the lady up and placed her on the mantel next to Pa's clock. Sure looked pretty there. So delicate. Dressed up the whole room, it did. Then she came and wrapped me in her arms.

''I never did see anything so beautiful, Maggie girl. Every time I look at her, I'll think of you.'' Then she pulled out her handkerchief and gave her nose a vigorous blow. ''But why did you do all this? Your Pa is right. Yourself and Johnny and the boy would have been enough.''

''Wanted you to know I wasn't forgetting you, Ma, even though I was far away.''

''You can't be doing these presents every visit, Maggie.''

I cast my face down. ''Don't know how many more visits there'll be, Ma. Johnny's mind's set to go further west this spring.''

I looked up at her and could see the pain in her eyes.

''How far west, daughter?''

''As far as there is, Ma. Clear to the Pacific Ocean in Oregon Country.''

She sat down in Pa's chair and kind of held onto the arms.

''But there's wild things there, and Indians. . . .''

''I know, Ma. But when his mind is set, it's set.''

''Like your pa—he's that way.'' She blew her nose again. ''Guess there's nothing to be done about it.''

'''Fraid not. But you are not to worry. We certainly won't set out this year yet. We're planning on working our way to the new city of Chicago, winter there, then maybe start for Independence in the spring. They set up wagon trains there, Ma. We wouldn't be going it alone. And in the meantime I'll just keep on with the letters. Don't know how it will be getting letters back beyond that, but I'll try, I surely will." I was sitting next to her now, kind of patting her arm.

"You are a good daughter, Maggie." She started to get up. "And now maybe you'd better help me start getting the supper together."

There was a good snow that night. Johnny and I watched it fall from the windows of my old bedroom before we climbed into the bed.

"Shouldn't last long. Just a little 'sound and fury, signifying nothing'," he said. "Sun will have it melted before tomorrow's out." He held me gently and watched some more.

It took two days for the sun to melt off the fields, then Johnny was out with Pa and the boys and Dickens, too, doing the final plowing and starting with the planting. We stayed for two weeks. I helped Ma around the house and watched how Jamie took up with Sarah and Charlie. Charlie soon had his little printing press operating and took great pride in setting up little bits of Bible verses for print, then presenting them to Pa to be read at suppertime. Pa tried not to show it, but I could see he was tickled by the thing. He sure had come around to the printed word a whole lot better than I'd ever wished for seven or eight years ago. Just goes to prove that even an old dog could learn new tricks, though I wouldn't exactly phrase it that way in front of Pa.

At the end of those two week, both Johnny and Jamie looked considerably better. They'd taken on a good ruddy color from working out in the open air, and I'd swear that Jamie had grown at least an inch. He was loving the farm, exploring every nook and cranny of it, hanging around the animals, begging to be allowed to try his hand at milking the cow and practically anything else. I watched this all a little wistfully. A farm sure was a good place for a growing child. Could Johnny and I offer him as much on the road? Finally the decision was out of my hands. Ma and Pa and the children all welcomed Jamie with open arms. I could see he'd fit in there real fine, and not be considered an outsider, but one of them. That mattered a whole lot.

The morning came when we were set to leave. We all shared breakfast kind of quietly. Pa pulled out the Bible and read the parable of the prodigal son. Then he looked up from the Book.

"It's not that I'll be casting aspersions on your life, Maggie and Johnny. Just want you to know that you'll always be welcome back here. No matter how things go for you out west."

"Thank you, Pa." Already had a lump in my throat and the worst still to come.

Then we started in to load up the wagon. Jamie helped us, then wanted to know where his mattress was. I stopped my work and kneeled down before him. Johnny sort of stood still in the background, knowing what was coming.

"Jamie, love. Johnny and I think you may be happier staying here on the farm with the children and the animals and all."

Tears welled up in his eyes. "You're never going to leave me, Mama and Papa, are you?" He looked slowly from one of us to the other, almost accusingly.

"But, Jamie. You love the farm."

He wiped his eyes. "Nice place to visit, a farm. Jamie goes with you. On the road." He stopped and looked into my eyes. "Please?"

"Oh, Jamie! Of course! We thought you wanted to stay."

Johnny was grinning in the background. "The boy wants to go, he goes."

Then we were all hugging each other, and Jamie and Johnny went to get the little mattress.

I looked up to find my Ma wiping her eyes.

159

"Boy knows who his mother is. That's a fine thing. You cherish him now, like he really was your own."

"Well, Ma. I guess he really is my own now." I smiled. "Came sooner than I planned, but maybe we'll have another sometime to give him company."

" 'The Lord works in mysterious ways. . . .' "

" 'His wonders to perform,' " I finished for her.

She looked at me. "You be careful of marauding Indians, now, and wild stampeding buffalo, and. . . ."

"Long time yet till we see any of those, Ma. Don't you start in on your worrying just yet."

"You'll learn, child, now you've got your own boy to look after. It's easier for a child to leave his parents than for the parents to watch the child go. You and your new family are never far from my thought and prayers. And your pa's, too, for that matter, though he never did speak out as much as I do."

I heard my pa clear his throat in the background and turned to him.

"Sometimes a woman can find words easier, Maggie. But if you all are set on going west, just remember to take your God with you. Maybe you'll be part of fulfilling the prophecy about 'when His dominion shall extend from the rivers to the ends of the earth'."

Then Johnny and Jamie were back with the final load and we were climbing on the wagon, Dickens raring to go.

My brothers and sister just kind of stared and the going was getting harder every minute. Finally Johnny gave the harness a shake and the horse was off.

"God go with you," called my father.

"I love you, all of you!" I yelled. Then I was reaching under my cape for my handerkerchief. Entirely missed the bend in the road with my eyes acting up like that.

We drove along an hour or two in total silence, then Jamie, sitting in the middle, gave me a tentative hug.

"Why are you so sad, Mama? We're on the road

again for sure. Going west like Papa wants. You should be happy." He looked at Johnny. "Right, Pa?"

"Right, Jamie. How about we stop right here and pull out your ma's banjo. Maybe she'll be giving you a few lessons if you ask her pretty."

So that's what we ended up doing. Started in with a fine old song that Joe Scraggs had taught us, about the earlier pioneers coming to the Ohio territory:

> Rise you up my dearest dear, and present to me your hand,
> And we'll all run away to some far and distant land.
> Where the ladies knit and sew, and the gents they plow and hoe,
> And we'll ramble in the canebrake, and shoot the buffalo.
>
> Come all ye fine young women who have got the mind to do,
> You can make us the clothing, you can knit and you can sew.
> We'll build you fine log cabins by the blessed Ohio,
> Through the wild woods we'll wander, and we'll chase the buffalo.

That kind of cheered us all up, then we went through practically our entire repertoire of songs the rest of that day. The sadness just kind of melted away, to be replaced by a feeling of excitement and anticipation of the unknown. After all, Ma and Pa and the boys were doing what they did best. In our own way, we were doing the same. Happy faces made the road shorter, and we did have a fair piece to travel in the getting west.

CHAPTER 11

WASN'T MORE THAN three hundred miles as the crow flies to Chicago. Since we weren't crows, it took us awhile longer to get there. 'Course if we'd been rich and in a great hurry, we could've done it in maybe a week—between the steamboats and the stage-coaches. Might've even been able to go for a piece on one of those newfangled railroads people were talking about. Heard they were working on putting one up in Illinois. Also heard they were even chancier than the steamboats, from the point of view of getting you somewhere in one piece. Looking at it that way, I guess it would've been an adventure for sure, although we'd still be missing out on the daily piece of anticipation, not knowing what was around the next bend or over that rise in the distance. As it was, it took clear into the autumn to cover those miles.

We went north for a while, taking our time with the bookselling, then finally crossed into the central part of Indiana. Flat as a pancake, it was. We went through the town of Lafayette and camped north of there in a bunch of woods called Tippecanoe. It was mighty impressive to be on the battleground where our late and lamented President William Henry Harrison defeated the Shawnee Indiana way back in 1811, making his reputation and chasing the poor Indians still further West, though from my understanding of it, a few of them were still around up to a dozen years ago before they gave up and crossed the Mississippi River.

From there we moved on to a little town named Kokomo after the Indian chief. It was a pleasant enough little place and we decided to stay a few days and stock up on supplies. I guess we'd backtracked some from Lafayette, but we were always going off on new little tracks or roads, curious as to where they might lead.

Well, to make a long story short, we barely had tied Dickens up to the post of the general store when we bumped into a long funeral procession wending its way down the main street. Looked like it must've been a well-loved person, by the size of the parade of mourners following the plain wooden coffin. Come to find out it was the local schoolmaster had passed on at an elevated age. The townspeople had already sent a letter off to Cincinnati in search of a replacement, but expected none for at least a month.

Johnny got to talking to the mayor, a Mr. Hines, who'd been casting glances at the writing on the side of our wagon. Before you knew it, Johnny had agreed to stay and take over the schoolhouse in the interim. Told the mayor I could help as well, since I was "an expert" at teaching youngsters to read. Well, you could've knocked me over with a feather at that, but since we really weren't in any great hurry, seemed no harm in the trying, especially since Johnny also talked the mayor into restocking the schoolroom with books from our wagon.

So there we were in Kokomo for the duration. Set up housekeeping in the little two rooms built for the master behind the schoolhouse. Jamie thought it was a fine adventure. He got to sit in the schoolhouse for eight hours a day with the little ones, and play at school. I guess you could say that's what Johnny and I were doing, too. Johnny taught the older ones geography, which he said they were woefully lacking in, not to mention Shakespeare and other fine authors. I got to test *McGuffey's Primers* and *Ray's Arithmetics* on the younger ones.

We were welcomed into the community real friendly-like. Attended the local church on Sundays and got to socialize at the covered-dish luncheons afterwards. It was pleasant talking to young mothers, learning that their daily problems were much like mine.

Jamie took to running off with a pack of boys about his age. They'd go down to the swimming hole just outside the town soon as school was out for the day. I kind of tagged along the first few times, making sure there wasn't any rough stuff from the older boys. Also, I wasn't quite sure of the swimming business. But Jamie took to that water like a fish. Before you knew it, he was swimming better than all of them.

I figured he must be going on five. (No telling when his birthday truly was, but Johnny and I had decided to celebrate it two days before Christmas, in honor of the day we'd found him.) Felicity enjoyed running along after Jamie, too. And when he'd get out into water she felt was too deep, she'd let off a noisy baying, and sure enough, Jamie would listen. Since Felicity had taken to watching over him, I'd let Jamie off on his own. That gave me some time to tend to the cooking and the laundry.

Well, that month kind of slid into six weeks till the new schoolmaster finally turned up day before the Fourth of July. We were all good and ready to move on by then, our bookstocks having been considerably depleted and our period of "civilization" whetting our appetites for the road again. But we had to stay and celebrate the Fourth. Jamie was looking forward to beating a drum in the band, and Johnny's and my instruments and voices were expected to help liven up the picnicking for the rest of the day.

And it surely was a day! The whole town was there, flags waving from most every hand. We'd had the school children build and paint a little statue of George Washington out of paper and glue to be placed in the center of the town square. Then, of course, we'd taught the children patriotic songs for a little concert. Luckily that went over well, especially the new number, "Columbia, the Gem of the Ocean," out from the East. Would've thrown in "The Tippecanoe Quick Step" as well, but left it out as unseemly, considering President Harrison hadn't managed to live very long into the current administration. Afterward, Johnny gave a pretty little speech about celebrating the Fourth. He quoted some from President John Adams:

> I am apt to believe it will be celebrated by succeeding generations as the great anniversary festival . . . solemnized with pomp and parade, with shows, games and sports, guns, bells, bonfires and illuminations, from one end of this continent to the other, from this time forward forevermore.

Then Johnny sprung the little joke. "Of course, friends, President Adams was referring to the *Second* Day of July, the day when the Continental Congress approved a resolution of independence, and not the *Fourth*, when Congress approved the Declaration of Independence and it was signed. Just goes to prove that even Presidents of the United States of America can make a little mistake now and again!"

He waited for the chuckle from the crowd, and after he'd gotten a good one, he turned the proceedings over to Mayor Hines, who started up the sports with the greased-pole climbing. Most all of the local young men took part in that, and my, did they end up messy!

Grease from forehead to toes! Of course, then they were all set for the greased-pig catching. And after they'd cleaned themselves up from *that* event, they got down to business with the pie contest, seeing who could swallow the most.

Jamie wanted to know why he couldn't take part in that one, since he figured he could eat just about as much pie as anyone else. Then his little friends, standing around listening, wanted to be part of it as well, so finally they took a few pies and had a junior and senior pie-eating contest. I wasn't too pleased, because I knew that the results would be nothing more than a nasty stomachache, but there was little I could do about it.

Come nighttime, Jamie's stomach had settled down again and he was in fine fettle for watching the fireworks and the shooting off of a little cannon someone had hauled clear over from Tippecanoe years back. Kept it all shiny in front of the mayor's house most of the year, only pulling it out for major occasions like the Fourth. By the time I dragged Jamie off to bed, not without some whimpering, half the men in town were roaring drunk. Johnny shrugged his shoulders at the sights and commented as how the Fourth of July *was* a volatile occasion, but nevertheless it had been a bang-up day. A fitting conclusion, Johnny observed, to a bang-up day—start to finish!

When we got into that wagon the next day, stuffed almost to the rim with bread and pies as farewell presents from the town, you'd think we'd set off to the north and Chicago. Not at all.

Johnny had heard from an oldtimer in the town about something called Indian "mounds" about fifty miles to the south and east. Johnny got it into his head to visit those mounds, so south we went. Nearly a week later we were traveling through mostly flatlands when suddenly these little hills started popping up around us—curious things, almost like someone had built them up on purpose. Johnny kind of grinned at the sight, then pulled up to the nearest one and unharnessed Dickens for a rest.

"Well, I figure these are the mounds, Meg."

"These little hills?"

"Yes. Sacred to the Indians, they were." He stretched and walked around looking, then bent over and returned to place something in my hand.

"What is it?"

"Looks like a flint arrowhead to me."

I shivered. "Sure its owner isn't skulking somewhere around?"

"Nope. Most likely he's buried in the mound."

"You mean this is a graveyard, Indian style?"

"That's my thinking on the subject."

"Well, let's travel on and leave them in peace. Had enough hard luck from our kind as it is."

By then, though, Jamie had let out a whoop and came running over to show us another arrowhead he'd found. That was the end of our traveling for the day.

I sighed and started in rounding up wood for a campfire to make some dinner. Jamie, my usual gatherer, was off searching for more arrowheads with his father. That went on all afternoon until they had a little pile of treasures near the wagon—a lovely little Indian pot with corn cob designs pressed into its side, and about a dozen arrowheads, not to mention what looked to be the head of a hatchet.

I just shook my head and fed them their supper. Both of them were pleased as punch, but when they wanted me to sleep with them outside the wagon that night, I decided on the bunks. As it was, I kept waking up thinking I was hearing a kind of ghostly tom-tom beating. Come morning, they scoffed at my dreams, but finally loaded the wagon and we headed off north again.

167

In mid-September we wandered into Chicago. And we weren't alone on the road, either. The closer we got, the more wagon loads of grain we came up against, their drivers all making for the funny-looking buildings we later learned were called "elevators." They were springing up on the shores of the Des Plains River right up to Lake Michigan itself, where steamboats came to pick up the grain and start the long haul back East. If it were Cincinnati I was expecting, I'd have been in for a shock. Luckily I was geared up for a smallish place. Wasn't quite ready yet for the combination of speculators, land boomers and assorted riff-raff that had gathered there from seemingly all over the compass.

It was a mudhole for sure, and my pa would've been mightily put out by the hard drinking and otherwise wild living that seemed to be going on. I didn't let on to much of this in my letters home. No point in giving the whole family the jitters, and Chicago only the armpit edge of the wilderness, so to speak. Heaven knew what lay beyond.

It was a bustling place. Maybe nearly twenty thousand souls by Johnny's figuring. And they were forward looking enough to be starting to lay in wooden sidewalks and planked streets. Hadn't made that much progress on it yet, though. And no matter what they put down, didn't seem to make much difference anyhow. Everything just sort of kept sinking into the soft mud the city was built on. Never could figure why people insisted on building cities in the middle of swamps. But Johnny said it was the "location" that counted. He figured the lakefront area would build up considerably in times to come.

Not that there wasn't enough sawing and hammering going on already. Frame buildings were going up everywhere, and they'd no sooner have a face on them before the signs would go up: "Attorney-at-law" this or that (Chicago seemed to have an

168

overwhelming number of lawyers, maybe to keep the peace between the riff-raff); dry goods stores with pretty calico and striped ticking and red and blue flannels in the windows; barrooms; land offices; even theaters and churches and new hotels. Practically every church had a sign up proclaiming a "Season of Prayer." Must've been to try and combat all the sin poking about. Didn't seem to have a noticeable effect though, as far as I could tell during the period of our stay.

It didn't take long for Johnny to track down the handful of bookstores in that place for the restocking. They were mostly tucked in between other shops around Lake and Clark Streets, the main thoroughfares. Then he located a print shop-newspaper combination and soon talked himself into a wintering job.

That left Jamie and me to explore the city together, as far as Lake Michigan. Jamie and I enjoyed that lake and took to fishing for our supper in it until it got too cold.

Then we tried to find a decent boarding house where maybe we could help out, like last year at Mrs. Ziegler's. That took some doing. But there were a few decent folks coming up to settle, and we finally got us a place with a Mrs. Wentworth, another widow lady. Seemed like widow ladies had little else to do to protect themselves once their husbands had gone. Never did stay at a boarding house that wasn't run by one.

Soon enough found out that the late Mr. Wentworth had been a gambler, much to his wife and children's regret. Got himself killed in an argument over a card game one night. But Mrs. Wentworth swore up and down that he'd been a fine provider when his luck was on. Even won the "balloon" boarding house, as they called them in Chicago, that we were staying in. I made no comment except to myself, along the lines of the Lord's looking after idiots and orphans. He'd also left seven little Wentworths and they stormed about the house, always up to some devilment. Jamie would've been storming right after them if I'd let him, but I didn't.

Talked about it to Johnny, serious-like one night after we'd been there about a week. "Young Jamie's going to lose all of his upbringing if we allow him loose in this household all winter."

"A child's got a right to be a child on occasion."

"Not if the other children are as wild as these Wentworths."

He sighed. "All right, then. What do you suggest?"

"Isn't there a school we could be putting him in? And you were saying they could use another good typesetter at the paper. Wouldn't I do? You told me once my hands were perfect for it. And I'd be learning that trade to help you later when we need it out west."

"You're right about all that, Meg, but a woman's place is not in the print shop."

"Don't see why not. And I can for sure tell you that my place is not here, either. Sometimes two women in the kitchen can ruin the broth. That's the way it is with Mrs. Wentworth and me—she's not Mrs. Ziegler."

"I noticed. Dinner last night was kind of hard to swallow, and then it just sort of sat there, like a rock or something."

"I'd be delighted to give her suggestions, but she's not the type to take to them. Please, Johnny! Will you talk to your boss about me?"

He sighed again. "All right, Meg. I'll see what I can do."

So the next morning after breakfast, he set off to work with a worried expression on his face. I could tell he'd do his duty by me, but he certainly wasn't keen on it. For myself, I took young Jamie in tow and left to find the nearest schoolhouse. I'd already learned they'd had free schools in Chicago for almost three years now. Might as well be taking advantage of the learning possibilities.

Well, the first school we walked into I knew at once wouldn't do. About forty children were lounging around in their straight-backed seats, balancing slates on their laps and throwing spit-balls at the thin and obviously overwrought schoolmaster in front of the room. I gave Jamie's hand a tug and hauled him right out of there. Whilst he thought it looked like fun, I had different ideas about education.

We spent that whole blessed day traipsing around the city looking for a suitable school. We were about to go back to the boarding house in total frustration when I came upon the sign in front of a church a few streets over from Mrs. Wentworth's. It said "A few suitable students are being sought for our school. Greek and Latin tutoring included." I looked at the sign, then down at Jamie. Why not at least look? Nothing else had proved suitable. So we walked into the small, rather nondescript building next ot the church, and I was soon face to face with a gentle-looking man. I stood staring at him for a moment.

"I am Father Feeney. May I help you and the boy in any way?"

His voice was pleasant, but he had an air of authority about him.

"Well, sir, my boy Jamie and I were wondering about your school."

He looked at Jamie. "The lad seems a bit young."

"He's close to five near as we figure it, sir. He's been adopted, you see. . . . And he already knows how to read and figure. He's got a quick mind and needs something to fill it up and keep him out of mischief for the winter."

"I am delighted that you have come to talk to me about his education. Let's just see what he can do." He led us into a booklined room, chose a volume,

171

then put it on the big desk near the fireplace. "Come here, Jamie, and read a bit for me."

It was the Bible. Looked lots like my pa's and it made me feel good. Jamie opened it up to Jonah and started to read out in his clear little voice, only stumbling now and again. Then he finished the chapter about the whale and stopped.

"Why do you suppose God let that whale swallow Jonah, young man?"

Jamie thought for a minute. "Guess He figured Jonah needed some convincing, sir."

Father Feeney laughed. "Close enough." He looked at me. "My mission here is to teach, and with God's help, I've been successful. I'd be happy to include your son in my classes, if you are willing."

"That sounds wonderful. Let me talk it over with his father tonight."

Then we were ushered out of the quiet house.

Johnny and I had a serious talk that night, after Jamie had fallen asleep. I told him about the school situation, and Father Feeney.

"Well, what do you think?"

"It's a big, new country, Meg. And there's no telling what kind of people we'll meet further West. If this Father Feeney can give our Jamie teaching based on the Bible, he'll be better grounded, no matter what challenges may meet him. And the Greek and Latin . . . " He looked a little wistful. I knew he was thinking that he'd have liked to have had the opportunity to learn those very things himself.

"Then it's all right?"

"Yes. We'll give it a chance."

I snuggled closer to his warm body. "And what about me, Johnny? What did your boss say?"

"Well . . . he wasn't overwhelmed with joy at the idea. But he said he'd give you a week's chance. . . ."

"Johnny!"

"Hush. A week's chance to prove yourself at no pay. After that, if you work out, he'd pay you three dollars a week, same hours as mine."

"But, Johnny! You're getting six a week this winter, and you started out at four dollars a week last year. . . ."

"Don't go complaining, girl. There's no way for me to tell him what a good worker I know you are. Women don't get paid the same as men, no matter how you look at it."

"That's not fair!" I spit out indignantly.

"Maybe not, but that's the way it is in this year of our Lord 1844."

"Well, I'll show him a thing or two, anyway, about how I can work as well as a man. Leastways at typecasting."

He looked at my determined expression, laughed, then kissed the look from my face. "I believe you will, Meg. But I'll have to keep a close harness on you or next thing you know you'll be wanting to vote like a man as well."

I was about to querulously inquire what was so terrible about *that* idea when I looked at his face and decided I'd gotten enough concessions for the night. No point in trying to overstretch the bounds of a man's mind. They could only handle so much at a time.

So then Jamie was off in school and I was liberated from Mrs. Wentworth's kitchen and bedmaking to start in at the print shop. I will say that there were times during that first week when I thought sure my back would break from the bending over the type cases. But I was determined not to be shown up. Got enough snickers behind my back from the other workers about the place, including the boss, who figured I'd give in for sure by week's end. But I didn't give in. Just worked harder. By the end of that week I figure I was actually becoming useful around the place.

They started me off working on simple things, like setting up broadsheet advertisements. Pretty soon I was moving on to sheet music. The fact that I could actually read the notes, thanks to Mr. Mueller last winter, was a big factor in my favor. Nobody else there could, except Johnny, who was busy working one of the big presses. Hate to see how those notes would've come out otherwise.

Finally it was late Saturday afternoon. I was putting away type when the boss called me over to his little cubbyhole.

"Yes, sir?"

"Well, Mrs. Stuart, I guess you can stay if you really have a mind to."

"Yes, sir. Thank you, sir!"

"Now, mind you, I won't have any slacking off. Keep up your improvements and you'll have pay in your hand end of next week."

"Yes, sir."

Then he dismissed me with a nod of his head and I went waltzing across the grimy floor of the plant feeling seven feet tall. Soon it was quitting time and I went home with Johnny, ate my dinner, listened to Jamie chatter for a bit, then crashed into my bed and slept for a full twelve hours. Johnny had to shake me awake hard in time for church the next day.

And so it went, week after week. I had become as pale as Johnny by this time, and Jamie was acting a little neglected. He'd try to cheer us up nights by conjugating Latin verbs for us. "*Amo, amas, amat,*" was his favorite. I appreciated the thought involved but was just too worn out by the twelve house of work to brighten up much. Finally, when it was nearly Christmas, Johnny made me stay awake one night to talk.

"What exactly are you trying to prove, Meg, and to whom?"

"Whatever are you talking about, Johnny?"

"You know full well what I'm referring to, girl. You wanted to learn how to typeset. You did. You wanted to work like a man. You are. Unfortunately you are no longer acting or feeling like the girl I married. Jamie and I are both feeling neglected. You come home dog-tired, fit for nothing but a mouthful of food and sleep. You've gone away from us, Meg, and we miss you!"

The last was said with a plaintiveness even I could not ignore.

"What do you want me to do, Johnny?"

"Stop the job. The three dollars a week aren't worth losing you."

"You know I can't give up like that, Johnny."

"It's not giving up. You proved what you wanted to prove. Stop now, please."

I made him no answer to that, but just sort of crawled up into my side of the bed, back turned to him. The good Lord knew I'd had enough long since, but my stubborn red-headed pride wouldn't let me free. I heard Johnny sigh a long sigh, then blow out the candle.

The next day, events were taken out of my hands. I woke up feeling mighty poorly and vomiting. Johnny rushed me to a doctor who gave me a good looking over, then finally smiled.

"You've got no signs of cholera or any other sickness, Mrs. Stuart. I do believe you are pregnant!"

Johnny had been sitting there with a worried expression on his face. Now he lit up all over and put a protective arm around my shoulder.

"What would you recommend, Doctor?"

"Well, she is a little peaked. I'd recommend a lot of bedrest for a few weeks, then just take everything a little easier. She's basically a sturdy woman, just needs a little feeding up.''

''Thank you, doctor.'' Johnny paid the fee gratefully and took me home to bed.

''You heard what the doctor said, woman. There'll be no more print shop for you. I expect a nice healthy child in six or seven months.''

''Yes, Johnny,'' I said with more relief than anything else. ''Just hand me the Bible before you go back to work. I guess it's time I caught up on my reading.''

Jamie was delighted, coming home from school and finding me there. He'd crawl up on the bed next to me and go over what he'd learned. Then we'd play little games together. By the day of his birthday celebration I was in pretty fine fettle. I got permission to use Mrs. Wentworth's kitchen and baked him up a batch of very special gingerbread cakes. And when Johnny came home from work we had a private celebration in our room. Johnny had brought a little parcel for the boy and Jamie opened it up with excitement in his eyes. It was a little toy covered wagon, pulled by a team of four oxen. The wheels really turned and the oxen could be unharnessed. Jamie forgot all his fine lessons and turned little boy again, playing the drover leading his team and wagon West, like we were planning on doing in the spring, loading and unloading the tiny kegs of supplies from the wagon. Maybe we had been pushing the education too hard. It sure was pleasant seeing him act like a child now and again.

Two days later it was Christmas. I'd gotten Johnny a new shirt made from some of that handsome blue flannel I'd been admiring in the dry goods stores. And Jamie had needed an entire new set of clothes. He'd clean grown out of last Christmas' set. Johnny presented me with two pretty lengths of cloth for making some ''expecting'' dresses, and Jamie gave me a bouquet of paper flowers he'd obviously labored long and hard over. We spent the day quietly, letting Jamie do the honors of reading the story of our Lord's own birth. I felt a pleasant closeness to His mother Mary, now that I was with child as well. I really knew how she felt for the first time, traveling all that way to Bethlehem and not being able to find a house for over their heads. Felt kind of the same way about my family. I sure hoped Johnny planned on a house of our own once we got to the Oregon country.

And so the rest of the winter passed by. I was growing in girth daily, and Johnny and Jamie both were happy about it. Jamie was looking for a little brother to play with. I warned him gently that odds were even that it might just be a girl child, but he pooh-poohed that thought. I just smiled. Whatever came, we'd get used to it mighty quickly.

When the worst of the winds and snowstorms that blew across Lake Michigan finally let up, we all started to sniff the air, waiting for the first telltale signs of spring. Finally Johnny decreed that we'd leave April first, no matter what. We had all had enough of Chicago by then, and were chafing at the bit for the leaving.

I'd received our annual letter from my pa, not saying a whole lot, but letting us know the family was all fine and thanking me for the weekly letters. He'd sounded delighted at the possibilities of a grandchild, and added a whole page of advice from my ma. Made me feel good to know everything was all right at home. Also made me wish we could manage a trip back before leaving. Unfortunately, that was out of the question, and I knew it well enough not to even bother Johnny with it.

He had a lot of other things on his mind, worrying about the money's reaching far enough to buy us a covered wagon and oxen, not to mention the travelling supplies we needed: one hundred fifty pounds of flour, fifty pounds of bacon, a keg of prunes, ten pounds of lye soap, a rifle and ammunition, to start with. He hadn't taken the step yet of deciding to abandon our book wagon. I think he was trying to figure out how to manage both. And nothing further had been said about the heavy, expensive printing press that we still could not afford.

I paid a visit to Father Feeney the day before we left, to thank him for his fine care of Jamie. He said he hated to see the boy go—that he'd never met a finer scholar that young. He presented Jamie with a Latin grammar as a parting gift and Jamie shook his hand formally, thanking him as well and promising to write when we'd reached Oregon. The teacher asked then if he might be permitted to give us a parting blessing. The way I figured it, we couldn't ever get enough of God's blessing, so I smiled yes. He laid a hand on each of us, saying it was an old Irish prayer:

> May the road rise to meet you,
> May the wind be always at your back.
> May the sun shine warm upon your face,
> the rains fall soft upon your fields.
> And until we meet again,
> May God hold you in the palm of His hand.

The words and his rich use of them were so sweet that I almost cried. I pulled Jamie out the door before I'd have to use my handkerchief, stopping only to say thank you again. That blessing stayed with me, and I often thought about it during the hard days ahead.

CHAPTER 12

COME APRIL FIRST we all piled into the wagon and headed out of Chicago. Couldn't help noticing the difference between the leavetaking here and at Cincinnati last year. Oh, Mrs. Wentworth said goodbye, and so did the seven little Wentworths, but I sure did miss Mrs. Ziegler's comfortable, motherly presence and concern.

I'd been thinking about her a lot lately, and finally sent off a little letter to her telling about Jamie's progress, and the new baby expected, and how we missed her clean home and cooking.

This letter-writing business was funny. Once you got into the habit, there was no stopping a person, even with no reasonable expectations of a reply. Just like you were sending thoughts off into the void, and maybe they would settle down and land where you hoped, and pass on a little consideration and love. It sure was hard leaving everything you knew for the unknown—even if the known was only a scrambling, dirty little place like Chicago.

Well, we made it out of the environs of the city and

settled down to clopping along a muddy pike, heading always south and west. I felt fine by this time. I figured I was maybe about five and a half months along with the baby. No more queasiness in the mornings. Johnny said I was positively blossoming. It was good to feel that my body was busy doing something useful the whole time I was sitting there, just traveling along.

Two days out of Chicago, we learned we'd been a little precipitate in leaving our winter haven. About noon the sun clouded over and snow began to fall. Not gentle snow, either. It was an icy, bitter snow, that banged against us and the wagon. From the looks of the darkening sky it wasn't going to be any passing fling, either. Johnny shoved Jamie and me inside the wagon where we rocked uncomfortably on the bunks, listening to the sharp sound of the snow pellets against the wagon sides while Johnny tried to find us a safe place to stop. Went on like that for an hour or two till we felt Dickens and the wagon grind to a halt. Johnny poked his head inside, looking like a frigid ice statue.

"Found us a farmhouse. You two stay put until I try to scare up the farmer and see about our welcome."

Jamie was off the top bunk in a flash, trying to peer through the little ice-covered window next to the stove.

"Can't see anything, Mama. Sure hope Papa can find his way back to us."

"Don't worry, Jamie. He will."

We waited what seemed like an awfully long time until Johnny came back. Then he climbed inside to talk to us.

"Seems to be some problems here, Meg. I finally found the farmer out in the barn, lying near his bull. Looks like the bull acted up some and gave him a good kick. He's passed out with a broken leg near as I can figure it. Can't find anyone up in the big house, either.'' He paused to wipe the snow out of his eyes. ''What do you figure we ought to do?''

''Well, gracious, Johnny, for starters we'd better get the poor man to his house and see about his leg.''

''He's a big man, and it'll take some doing. I don't want you lifting, Meg.''

''Jamie will help as well. We'll manage.'' The two of them looked at me. ''Well, don't just stand there. Get moving!''

I wrapped my cape around me good and tight and pulled the hood over my head, then bustled out. From the corner of my eye I saw Johnny shake his head a little, then follow. Holding tightly to each others' hands we made it to the barn. The farmer must've been unconscious for some time, because the cows were mooing like they needed a milking. Poor creatures would have to be patient for a bit yet. I looked down at the farmer. He was a big man, all around. Tall and fat, with a little bit of grizzled salt-and-pepper hair on the top of his head. I knelt down and felt the leg that was slightly askew, then ripped up his trouser leg to have a better look.

''We'd better set it right here, Johnny. See if you can find some bits of straight wood.''

Johnny and Jamie prowled about, then returned with a few usable pieces. Meanwhile I'd been ripping some pieces of cloth from the bottom of my petticoat. I'd always known there had to be a good reason why women wore petticoats, and now I figured I'd found the answer.

I wrapped up the leg and, between us, we managed to shove the poor man into a big wheelbarrow sitting empty nearby. Then it was just a matter of Johnny wheeling him up to the house. Well, in an hour or so we had a mattress near the fire, had the fires primed up some, and I was wiping his face with a damp cloth while Johnny was out tending to the stock. Slowly he started coming around.

His first words were, "Thank God you're back, Maeve." Then he looked at me.

"You're not my old woman. . . . Who are you?"

"Just a stranger passing through, looking for shelter from the storm."

"Look closer to an angel to me. Sure I'm not dead and gone to heaven?"

"I'm sorry, sir. But you are quite alive. I've got you by your kitchen fire, with a broken leg."

He looked down, tried to move both legs, then winced with pain.

"Ornery old bull's been trying to do me in for nigh on ten years now. He sure chose his moment, with the wife off to attend out daughter's birthing fifty miles away and gone." He winced again, then, "Whoever you are, I thank you. But what about my animals?"

"My husband is out tending them, sir."

He looked relieved. "I be Jonas Jackson, and I praise the Lord for sending you and yours in my time of need."

I completed the introductions, then asked if I might have the run of the kitchen to prepare some broth for him.

"Glory, yes! My house is yours, woman. Do whatever needs doing." Then he drifted out again.

Well, the storm passed in two days, but we ended up staying two weeks. Wasn't any other choice in the matter. I took over the house, and Johnny and Jamie the barn chores.

Jonas Jackson healed slowly and spent most of his days sitting stiffly by the fire, grumbling mildly about his affliction and wondering how the plowing and planting were to be done. Johnny and Jamie were just working up to get a start on it when the absent Maeve reappeared. She came clattering into the yard in a little buggy one day, all white hair and energy. When she saw her husband's sorry state, she flung up her arms, then got down on her knees and thanked the Lord for looking after Jonas. He was still calling me "Angel" and there was no way I could dissuade him from it. A little embarrassing it was, but the thought was right sweet. We came to learn that her daughter's birthing had been difficult, but she'd finally delivered up twin boys, to her husband's delight.

"'Course that makes eight little ones in as many years, but they do have a sizeable farm to feed them off. . . .'" Maeve was taken to rambling on like that. But whilst she was talking she was always working at something.

We finally left the two of them with Maeve harnessing up two horses to start in the plowing and Jonas carving fancy designs on a crutch by the kitchen fire. He'd bought a few books from Johnny, but I suspected it was a gesture of thanks only. Jonas wasn't the type to be reading, even with time on his hands.

And we were off again, me with a new petticoat courtesy of Maeve. This time spring was coming a little stronger on the air. Well, the bookselling was going mighty well, and Johnny didn't want to travel too hard on account of my condition, so it wasn't till high summer that we finally hit upon the Mississippi River on the border between Illinois and Missouri. We started heading south along the river, looking for a good crossing place when I suddenly knew, sure as anything, that my time was nigh. It was just midmorning, and my whole body felt mighty strange.

"Better find us a resting place, Johnny," I let out in a quick burst.

He looked at me worriedly. "What is it, Meg, honey?"

"Baby's decided it's time to meet the world."

Well, he lit into poor Dickens, and the horse broke into a trot, not knowing what was going on, a little bewildered. I hung on for dear life, and Jamie hung onto me, a concerned expression on his face.

"It's all right, Mama. Papa will find us a doctor."

"Yes, dear, don't you worry about it."

I was worrying enough for all of us. Hadn't had any experience at birthing yet and in between holding my breath at the cramps and letting out little prayers for strength when they let up, I was not noticing the scenery much. So it was somewhat of a surprise when we headed to the top of a rise and saw a city spread out before us. Johnny reigned in Dickens and stopped one of the wagons going the other way.

"Can you tell us what that place is, Sir?"

"Mormon city of Nauvoo, Mister, but I wouldn't be going that way if it can be helped. Heap of trouble they got there ever since last summer when a mob killed their leader, Joseph Smith."

"Would they have a doctor there? My wife is due for childbirth."

The farmer looked at us closer then. "Surely would have, at that. Biggest city in Illinois. But they're fighting the state militia right now. If you can spare the time I'd travel further."

"I'm thanking you, sir, but we can't spare the time." And Johnny hurried Dickens on.

Then we were entering the city. More like a fortress from what I could see between my panting. Neat, though. Neat houses on neatly squared streets. Well planned out by somebody, not like Chicago. And there was a huge building, kind of like a church, but bigger than any I'd ever seen before, with a golden statue of an angel blowing a horn on top. I took the angel as a good sign and got back to concentrating on the baby. Johnny stopped every so often and asked directions, then finally pulled up before a house.

"Doctor's supposed to live here," he said as he swung down and went to investigate. He returned a few minutes later with a tall, gray-haired man who *looked* reassuringly like a doctor, and they helped me off the wagon, into the house, and soon into a little room with a bed. The doctor shooed Johnny and Jamie outside and started in examining me.

"Looks like your husband got you here in the knick of time, Missus. I can see the baby's head already. Now when I say push, you *push*! Understand?"

"Yes, sir!"

Well, it still took considerably longer than I would've liked, but finally baby arrived. The doctor cleaned it up, then presented me with a beautiful little girl.

"Well done, Missus. She's a fine one, and a crop of red hair like I've never seen before." He looked at the rest of me closely then. "Just like yours!"

I took that baby and felt closer to heaven than I ever had. I'd been secretly wishing for a girl, and I guess the Lord had heard me even though I'd not had the nerve to put words to my thoughts.

"Please . . . my husband and son. . . ."

"I'll be getting them now."

Then Johnny and Jamie were crowding around, admiring the two of us. They both looked pleased as punch, and not a word from them about its being a girl, either. We'd already decided that whatever the baby ended up, it would be named after Johnny's father. Charlotte kind of smiled up at us—sort of like she approved of her name when I whispered it—then burrowed down looking for some refreshment.

The doctor ushered my men out, saying I could stay the night to regain my strength. I fell asleep in exhaustion, with Charlotte beside me.

From what I pieced together later, July thirteenth had been one amazing day for all of us. Johnny and Jamie had left me and baby Charlotte and gone to look for someplace to buy their suppers. Along the way they passed the printing shop where a little paper was put together. It was on the street right next to the river, kind of overlooking the Mississippi from an elevated position, almost like a little cliff. They'd hardly got past when a mob of angry men came tramping down the street, murder in their eyes, as Johnny put it. Johnny and Jamie crouched safely out of sight and watched as these men beat down the doors and windows of the shop yelling things he couldn't catch or understand. They manhandled the printers, then lugged the press out of the shop, and just flung it over the parapet into the river. Then, looking mighty pleased with themselves, the mob dispersed. Hearing the story, I could just see the speculative look in Johnny's eye. He had a bead on a printing press, for sure, and it was highly unlikely that any of these besieged Mormons was about to pull it out of the river anytime soon. Leave it longer that that and it would be a pile of rusted iron junk. A fine Ramage portable is was, too. He'd spotted that instantly from the distance. Couldn't be wrong with that pretty little brass finial glinting on the top. Not more than fifteen years old, either, and light for its kind—only seven or eight hundred pounds.

Well, come midnight, Johnny, Jamie, and the horse and wagon came skulking back along the lower shoreline beneath the parapet. Luckily it was a dark night. Johnny pulled off his clothes and dove into the water. Took four or five dives till he located the press, close into the shoreline. Then he went back with some strong rope, tied it on, and got Dickens to haul it up. Luckily, they were down below the ramparts of the city, and I guess there weren't many people brave enough to be prowling about these nights considering how the other locals felt. Right then and there Johnny dismantled the press bit by bit, drying it real good (as I later found out it was our sheets he used for that— never did get most of the grease stains out of them). Don't know how he managed it, but he and Jamie got the parts into the wagon. Not that they were that big, just very heavy. By then the moon had come out of the clouds, and Johnny was itching to get off of that beach. He finally got Dickens harnessed up again, and they scuttled off to a safe distance from town.

When they came to pick me up the next afternoon, I was mighty surprised to see another horse harnessed up next to Dickens. Johnny introduced the mare as "Sally," then when we were clear of Nauvoo explained the presence of the hew horse—to pull the extra weight of the wagon.

"Took some doing to round her up, too, Meg. All the city folk are selling everything in sight, pouring all their money into livestock. Seems their new leader, Brigham Young, is planning on clearing them all out of Illinois as soon as possible."

"But that's a big city full of people, Johnny. Where will he take them?"

"Heard mutterings about going so far West nobody would ever bother them again."

I blanched at the thought of transporting that many people through the wilderness. It was going to be hard enough for us, with a new baby and all. I settled down more comfortably in the bed pillows Johnny had arranged on the wagon seat for us and bent my head to admire baby Charlotte. She was sleeping nice as you could please, cradled in a big shawl I'd carefully wrapped around my shoulders and neck. Seemed as if she liked the slow jogging of the horses. That was very lucky. She'd have a lot more of it yet afor she grew up to walking size.

Of course, when we stopped to camp for the night, I finally had a look inside the wagon and let out a groan. Bits and pieces of the Ramage press cluttered up the entire living and walking space.

"Johnny! However are we going to manage traveling like this?" I wailed.

"Never you mind, Meg. Jamie and I will sleep

outdoors when the weather's fine. And I've rigged up a nice little hammock for Charlotte." He pointed to the bits of rope and cloth hanging down in the middle of everything. "It won't be forever, sweetheart."

"Well, I guess the Lord does help those who help themselves, Johnny, but I never did expect you to help yourself to a printing press."

He looked crestfallen. "Didn't steal it, Meg. Just found it, like."

"Well, you'd better be thanking the Lord for His bounty, then, and asking Him to help those poor people find their own land. They deserve that much, at least."

"Already done that with Jamie last night, although the boy was probably more asleep than awake over the prayers." Johnny gave another big yawn then, and I could see that I wasn't the only one good and tired.

"How far is it to Independence, Johnny?"

"I figure about two hundred and fifty miles . . ."

"As the crow flies." I finished for him, smiling.

"Yes. We could make it in eight days if we were to go down to St. Louis and take a steamboat up the Missouri River. If we had the fare."

Charlotte let out a wail from her resting place on my stomach. I backed out of the wagon and sat down on a piece of grass, resting my back against a tree and began to give her her dinner, softly touching the curls Johnny had bequeathed to her red hair. Jamie was already piling up a stack of dry wood for the campfire. Johnny began to fuss around it, getting it going for the meal. We'd stopped on a meadow above the Mississippi and it was real pretty looking across its broad length. I surely did like a nice piece of water nearby. So relaxing to gaze upon. But we'd have to be crossing this river any day now. Soon as we found the nearest ferry.

"We're not going to make it west this year yet, are we Johnny?"

He sat back from his little fire. "Probably not, Meg. From our readings on the subject, little as there is to be had, it seems to be downright dangerous to give it a try any later than June. April would be better. You have to figure on the weather at the mountain passes on the other end. Sure wouldn't want to get snowed in up there, with the little ones."

I looked down at Charlotte, busily suckling away at the little bit of milk that was starting to come. "Without me and them, you could've been out there long since, Johnny."

He slowly stood up, walked over, then sat down beside us, gently moving a bit of hair away from my forehead. "What you say is true, Meg. But without you and the children, there wouldn't be much point, would there?" He touched my hair again, then Charlotte's downy soft head. "Men aren't strong on sentiment, Meg, at least an outward showing of it. Or maybe it's just me growing up without a mother. But I want you to know that I'll love you always. For you, and for the children you've brought to us, with the Lord's help."

My eyes kind of misted over. "Thank you, Johnny." And then Jamie spotted us and trotted over.

"Are we going to have supper tonight? I'm hungry!"

Well, it wasn't easy, but we managed to learn to live with the press. There were a lot of toes stubbed in that wagon and, once or twice, I even heard Johnny taking Adam Ramage's name in vain over his handy little machine, but we managed to continue along with the help of the new horse. Dickens seemed to be much taken with "Miss Sally" as we took to calling her. And Felicity wasn't sure what to think at first, but soon she was nipping Miss Sally's heels in a friendly spirit, helping to hurry her down the long roads. We took our time traveling across Missouri, and did a big

189

business with the books. Seemed like we were the only book peddlers to come through this way in some time.

The land was a lot like Ohio for a while, then it sort of settled out to long grassy plains as we got closer to Independence. Johnny said it would be plains for hundreds and hundreds of miles beyond, as well. Sure was hard to imagine the length and breadth of this amazing country. We met up with mostly nice folks the whole trip, and I was even beginning to start to like the idea of wintering over in Independence. Figured it would give us a head start on preparations for the spring.

It was late September when we pulled into the dusty, bustling town of Johnny's dream for so many years. We'd followed the Missouri the last few days, watching steamboats chug past us, fighting the currents and occasionally getting grounded on a bit of sandbank. Their decks were always piled high with all fashions of wagons, mules, horses, and piles of harness. Johnny said that Independence was the starting point for more than just the Oregon Trail. Wilderness men took off from there for their trapping parties, and there was a regular route along the Santa Fe Trail from there as well.

We had to jog a bit south from the Missouri at the steamboat landing to get to Independence, which was some miles from the river, then finally we arrived. Just driving through the long main street it seemed as if the whole place was one huge wagon-building establishment. That and cattle raising. Oxen were fattening on grass all along the rims of the settlement, filling up for the winter and the hard spring journeys ahead of them. We looked around wide-eyed at the activity, then I let out a gasp.

"Johnny! Over there, look!"

He looked. Sure as life it was a real Indian. Blanket round his shoulders, and feathers in his hair. Just walking nice as you please down the main street. It was a shock for sure looking at that proud, nomadic face and sun-darkened skin. I stared until I remembered my manners. After that it was easier. Indians all over the place, braves and squaws and papooses. We later learned that they mostly camped on the outskirts of Independence, trading animals with the immigrants heading West. Most of them were of the Kansas tribe, but there were also Foxes, with shaved heads and painted faces, and Shawanoes and Delawares, as we later learned their names, not to mention all their shaggy little ponies tied everywhere to fences and posts.

Jamie was fascinated almost beyond excitement, and it was no surprise to us when later in the winter he started in bringing home Indian friends to play with, and adopted the extra handmade bow and arrow of one of these friends, struggling daily to master its use. Some of the locals didn't seem to approve much of this mixing, but Johnny and I didn't mind. We were all God's children, after all. Kept Jamie busy and happy and there didn't seem any harm to it.

First thing we did after we got the sightseeing out of our systems was to rent a little one-room log cabin for the winter. Only furniture it came with was a wooden table and benches and a big bed, with a little trundle bed underneath. As Johnny didn't yet have the way with wood that my Pa had, we bartered some books for a little cradle for Charlotte from a nearby family whose children had grown out of its use.

Then, while I made the place as cozy as possible, Johnny started in to worry about the big trip and the books. Books especially worried him. Our stock was practically all sold out, and Independence hadn't graduated into a bookstore as yet. He finally sat down and wrote out a long list of titles with a letter and money that he sent off by steamboat to his favorite shop in Cincinnati. No matter how you looked at it, the books should make it to us before the leaving in April, and Johnny couldn't see going west without books. Nohow.

Then he started shopping around for a good wagon to carry the press and the traveling supplies. Wasn't long before he'd settled on one and had the horses haul it home to our backyard. It was shaped like the big old Conestoga wagons that used to come and haul grain from my Pa, but it was smaller and lighter. It was built to comfortably carry about 1500 to 2200 pounds. It could handle more, of course, but it wasn't considered wise to overload it and thus overtax the animals on the long trip. Then Johnny started in to caulk up its bottom with tar and wax, liked he'd learned listening to some of the old-timers sitting around the town. Had to make it waterproof for the fording of rivers. When he finished up with that, he started the same process on our book wagon. I hated to see the pretty paint all smeared up with the black pitch, but I figured it would probably be due for a good overhaul once we'd made it West anyhow.

After these preparations were completed, Johnny went and bought a rifle. He was a little leery of it, never having had the use of a firearm before, but he and Jamie would go out to the outskirts of town and practice on it till they got to be pretty fair shots. Even took me and baby out once to give it a try. It was kind of fun shooting at targets, but I hoped never to have to aim it at a living creature.

Charlotte was growing into a right pretty little thing. The men called her "Charley," but not me. Pretty name like she had ought to be used. I was glad now for the wintering time to give her a chance to sleep and grow properly. As the cold winds, winds like I'd never known, came sweeping in off the prairie, we settled into a daily routine. After breakfast, Jamie would have his lessons for an hour or two, then he was free to run off with his friends. Then I'd start in with dinner preparations, fuss with the baby, and make supper in the afternoon. After supper we'd have our Bible readings and prayers before tucking in for the night.

That's more or less how it went, until Jamie's Indian friends got curious about the lessons and started banging on the door about breakfast time. Since they were always hungry, I ended up feeding them as well. "Straight Arrow" and "Running Bear," as he called them, then started to just squat on the floor silently listening as we did the lessons. Well, I couldn't stand a whole lot of that, so before long they were sitting at the table and I was starting in on *McGuffey's Primer* with them.

This went on for a month or two and we were into December when one day, after the lessons were through and the boys had raced out into the snow, I heard a timid knock on the cabin door. Just Charlotte and I were there and she was sleeping. Johnny had gone off into town for supplies. So I opened the door and you could have blown me over with a feather. Standing there was a pretty Indian squaw, all wrapped up in blankets. She just stood there and I just stared until my common sense finally returned and I waved her in out of the cold.

She stood by the fire another few moments, then finally spoke. "You good woman. Teach Indian boys white man's words."

"Yes." What else could I say?

"Boys my sons. Is good for them to learn. I come thank." And she unwrapped her blankets and presented me with two fresh-caught rabbits.

"How wonderful!" I smiled. "Please, will you have something warm to drink with me?" I had been cooking up a pot of soup with some dried meat and the broth was always soothing and healthy.

She nodded her assent, then curiously walked around the small place peering at this and that, but touching nothing. She smiled when she saw Charlotte sleeping in her crib, and couldn't resist touching her red hair.

"Baby. Most pretty!"

"Thank you!" I was about to hand her a cup, but she made a beeline to the rabbits.

"Fur. Baby." She pointed. Then motioned to her hands. "Fur keep warm for baby."

"I touched a skin. It was thick with its winter coat, and soft.

"But how? How to cure skins?" I spoke slowly, hoping she would catch the meaning.

"Not know how?" It seemed hard for her to fathom. She thought of a minute. "My white name 'Flower Blossom.' I teach you."

Then she quickly drank her broth and went out the door, leaving me wondering.

True to her word, though, she reappeared the next day, with a small cloth full of tools, directly after the lessons. I had carefully removed the skins as best I could and presented them to her. She set them on the table and began showing me how to scrape and clean them properly.

That was the beginning of our friendship. She came then nearly every day, sometimes to listen in on the lessons as well, and soon her English came easier, although she still had trouble pronouncing "Meg." Johnny had started to practice with his rifle on small game to help feed us through the winter, and whenever a new skin was available we worked on it together. She liked to watch me cook, too, and soon we were comparing recipes like old friends.

I learned that her family belonged to the Kansas tribe. They were nearly destitute, living on their hunting and horse trading, caught between the worlds of the Indians and the white men who had pretty much taken over their ancestral lands. It was a sad state of affairs and I wasn't sure what to do about it, aside from trying to help her and her sons adapt.

It started out that way, but soon I found I was learning much from her as well, and truly enjoying her quiet company. The winter days would have dragged terribly without her. After the skins were cured, she taught me how to sew them together, and soon I had fur mittens for the whole family, who found them much warmer in this new kind of cold than their old woolen ones. Then we started in on moccasins for everyone's feet—her sons had already taught Jamie how to make and use wooden snowshoes, and soon the whole family, aside from Charlotte, of course, got into the habit of that as well. Kept your feet a lot drier, and made the walking easier, too.

So Christmas passed, and when it got close to the New Year, Johnny suggested we invite Flower Blossom's whole family for a little celebration. I presented her with the idea, and she was doubtful what her man would think, but promised to ask.

Well, we weren't sure what would happen, but come New Year's Day, I started in making preparations with the food anyhow. I'd been saving a few pumpkins from the fall, and made pies out of those, and also started up a big ham roast in the tin reflector oven Johnny had got for me. It was a right handy gadget, and saved the meat juices nicely at the bottom for gravy making. He'd said it was so light he didn't see why we couldn't take it with us.

Johnny had also invited a few of the bachelor men that had been so easy with giving him advice for the journey. Pretty soon they started arriving, bringing little presents like a piece of bacon, or a few potatoes, and fiddles to play. The last one, a big, full-bearded old man, who'd worn out most of his youth in the wilderness, brought a hand-made whistle for Jamie and a jaw harp to play himself.

Then our Indians arrived. And quite a sight they

were, too. Flower Blossom's husband, Big Snake, came in glory. His head was shaved and painted red, with the one tuft of hair left dangling eagle feathers and two rattlesnake tails. He had bright glass in his ears and a collar of grizzly-bear claws. Next to his sartorial splendor, everybody else just sort of faded into awed insignificance. He also brought a haunch of fresh deer, and this offering kind of eased his fierce looks somewhat.

Charlotte cried first time she saw him, but in a little while she was cooing in his lap, batting at his claw necklace. Funniest sight you ever saw. I'd heard Indians loved babies and children, but this made a believer out of me. His boys had brought some drums, and soon, with all the instruments in the tiny house, you could have heard us clear to Ohio. It was some party, and made me feel good about 1846. Seemed to me that with a little grace and the help of the Lord, a body could get on with just about anyone in this world.

As the winter began to fade away and the first green shoots started coming from the earth, Flower Blossom and I, with Charlotte strapped to my back, Indian fashion, would spend hours out in the fields. We exchanged information on herbs and their medicinal uses, and she taught me which roots were good to eat. The way she put it, the Great Spirit had put enough things on the earth so that no one ever had to starve if they could read His signs. By then I'd figured we were talking about the same God, only giving Him different names. There was comfort in that. There was comfort, too, in learning how to make Indian pemmican for traveling out of bits of dried meats, roots, berries, an a little animal grease. May not have been the tastiest stuff in the world, but if we hit a bad spot on our journey, my family wouldn't go hungry.

With the greening of spring came also the immigrants from the East. Hundreds of them started in arriving daily by river and land and took to camping on the plains just west of Independence, getting organized for the overland trip. Johnny went out daily, trying to choose a group he felt suitable to travel with. He'd come back with little bits and pieces of information we'd not thought of, then go into town to purchase more supplies. Finally he settled on a group in late March and took me and the children out one day to meet them and sit in on their "constitution making" as he called it. It struck me as funny at first, but made a whole lot of sense for those traveling together to make up their own rules and regulations for the period of the journey, which might take anywhere from four to six months.

First thing they did was elect a "captain" to be in charge. Out of a group of about a hundred men, women, and children in our party, they picked a big man named Joshua Chandler. He had a wife and six children, ranging in age from Charlotte's up to about twelve years. His loud voice was useful, but he wasn't overly boastful. He spoke about how we'd soon all be out of the territorial United States with no one to help us, aside from a few fur trading forts along the way. So we'd just have to help ourselves. Well, it took all day, but they made up and wrote down a whole list of do's and don'ts then made us all swear on the Bible that we'd follow his word as long as he didn't make any fearsome mistakes. If that happened, God forbid, we could elect another captain democratically. We also had to swear to give whatever aid we could to one another for the duration, like we were kin. We returned to our little cabin that night, having a powerful amount of respect for our forthcoming trip.

Johnny's books had arrived in March, along with my pa's annual letter, telling us that everyone was fine, as usual, and wishing us joy and a good Christian upbringing for Charlotte, which Pa sincerely wished we could do out in the "no man's land you are bound and determined to take yourselves off to." I shed my usual tears over that, and tried to read between the lines for all the other information I wished he'd written about. No telling how many years before I'd get another from my family.

When the day came to do our final packing of all of our earthly possessions into those two wagons, I certainly had my second thoughts, not that I'd speak of them to Johnny. He was too high in the sky, coming so close to his fondest dream. He went about the loading with a whistle and a song and an almost feverish expression on his face. And Jamie was just the same. That left me only Charlotte to whisper to, and the Lord, of course.

We were having our final meal in the cabin when Flower Blossom and her boys arrived to wish us farewell in their own way. I could see fine in her eyes that she wished she were going as well, but that would not have been contenanced by the other immigrants.

The boys made Jamie a present of the bow and arrows with which he'd played with them all winter. Flower Blossom put a string of wampum beads around my neck. Couldn't help noticing that it was her favorite one. I gave her and the boys several *McGuffey's* and all the pots and pans that were too heavy to travel with. Also gave her Charlotte's cradle, with the wish that she'd have a young one to fill it up soon. That made her real happy. Then we bade each other farewell, me with tears in my eyes, and her with the usual stoic Indian expression. Was mighty hard seeing them go out the door the last time. Like others we'd met along the way, they had become true friends.

I tried hard that night in bed not to think of those others we'd be leaving behind forever. My ma and pa and sister and brothers. Old Mr. Stuart and Mabel buried in Athens, Ohio. Hildy and her staunch German husband. Mrs. Ziegler and her boarders. Joe and Ingrid. Life sure was funny, putting you in the path of good people, then pulling you apart again. I was kind of snuffling in my pillow over it all when Johnny rolled over and put an arm around me.

"Don't fret, Meg. You'll not be leaving the children or me. And the Lord will be traveling with us. It's new adventures and people we're going to. We'll be part of that 'manifest destiny' people are talking about back East. And we'll be taking our knowledge and care and love with us to share."

I settled into his embrace.

And the next day we hauled our wagons out to meet the others on the plain. We had breakfast there with our new family. Captain Chandler read from the Bible. Joshua 1:9 it was, when Joshua was leading the Chosen People into the Promised Land: "Have I not commanded thee? Be strong and of good courage; be not afraid, neither be thou dismayed: for the Lord thy God is with thee withersoever thou goest." Then we all sang "Old Hundred" together and got into our wagons. The Captain yelled, "Wagons ho!" gave a crack of his whip, and we were off to the West. I didn't bother to look behind. I guessed that from this day forward, everything was ahead of us.

ABOUT THE AUTHOR

She might be called "a purveyor of books, educational and inspirational, moralistic and fanciful," but whatever the label, KATHLEEN KARR shares with the main characters in her latest novel a fascination with the printed word.

In addition to her writing, she finds time to teach (at local universities), to be involved in the exhibition end of the motion picture industry (with the Circle Theaters in Washington, D.C.), and to introduce her two growing children to a love of books. In fact, with the aid of a recently acquired set of *McGuffey's Readers*, Mrs. Karr is teaching her daughter Suzanne to read as Meg learned over a century ago.

This storybook family lives in a restored turn-of-the-century townhouse in Washington, D.C.

A Letter To Our Readers

Dear Reader:

Pioneering is an exhilarating experience, filled with opportunities for exploring new frontiers. The Zondervan Corporation is proud to be the first major publisher to launch a series of inspirational romances designed to inspire and uplift as well as to provide wholesome entertainment. In order that we might better contribute to your reading enjoyment, we would appreciate your taking a few minutes to respond to the following questions and return to:

Anne Severance, Editor
The Zondervan Publishing House
1415 Lake Drive, S.E.
Grand Rapids, Michigan   49506

1. Did you enjoy reading FROM THIS DAY FORWARD?
   ☐ Very much. I would like to see more books by this author!
   ☐ Moderately
   ☐ I would have enjoyed it more if _____

2. Where did you purchase this book? _____

3. What influenced your decision to purchase this book?
   ☐ Cover   ☐ Back cover copy
   ☐ Title   ☐ Friends
   ☐ Publicity   ☐ Other _____

4. Please rate the following elements from 1 (poor) to 10 (superior).

- ☐ Heroine
- ☐ Hero
- ☐ Setting
- ☐ Plot
- ☐ Inspirational theme
- ☐ Secondary characters

5. Which settings would you like to see in future Serenade Serenata Books?

_____   _____

_____   _____

6. What are some inspirational themes you would like to see treated in future books?

_____   _____

_____   _____

7. Would you be interested in reading other Serenade Serenata or Serenade Saga Books?

- ☐ Very interested
- ☐ Moderately interested
- ☐ Not interested

8. Please indicate your age range:

- ☐ Under 18
- ☐ 18–24
- ☐ 25–34
- ☐ 35–45
- ☐ 46–55
- ☐ Over 55

9. Would you be interested in a Serenade book club? If so, please give us your name and address:

Name _____

Occupation _____

Address _____

City _____ State _____ Zip _____

Serenade Saga Books are inspirational romances in historical settings, designed to bring you a joyful, heart-lifting reading experience.

Serenade Saga books available in your local bookstore:

Watch for other books in the *Serenade Saga* series coming soon:

Serenade Serenata Books are inspirational romances in contemporary settings, designed to bring you a joyful, heart-lifting reading experience.

Serenade Serenata books available in your local bookstore:

Watch for other books in both the *Serenade Serenata* (contemporary) series coming soon: